D0713103

IN PURSUIT OF LAVENDER

Anthem Press
An imprint of Wimbledon Publishing Company
www.anthempress.com

This edition first published in UK and USA 2013
by ANTHEM PRESS
75–76 Blackfriars Road, London SE1 8HA, UK
or PO Box 9779, London SW19 7ZG, UK
and
244 Madison Ave. #116, New York, NY 10016, USA

Original title: Tōbō kuso tawake
Copyright © Akiko Itoyama 2005
Originally published in Japan by Chuo Koron Shinsha, Tokyo
English translation copyright © Charles De Wolf 2013

A CIP record for this book is available from the British Library.

ISBN-13: 978 0 85728 046 6 (Hbk)
ISBN-10: 0 85728 046 5 (Hbk)

This title is also available as an eBook.

This book has been selected by the Japanese Literature Publishing Project (JLPP),
an initiative of the Agency for Cultural Affairs of Japan.

IN PURSUIT OF LAVENDER

Akiko Itoyama

Translated by Charles De Wolf

ANTHEM PRESS
LONDON · NEW YORK · DELHI

1

Twenty yards of linen are worth one coat.

I've been running and running but still can't shake off that voice. Knowing that it's an auditory hallucination doesn't help me put a stop to it. Even the doctors couldn't do that.

Twenty yards of linen are worth one coat.

I haven't a clue what it means, but when I hear it, I fall apart. Fretful, impulsive, I fall under the sway of a pitch-black throbbing, like a bicycle in the night that loses its brakes at the top of a mountain pass and goes careening down the slope.

It was high tide and Hakata Bay had surged back up the Hiikawa, the water reaching almost to the bridge planks. I was running along the narrow private road behind Seinan Gakuin Christian university, my back to the sea. I was not going back to the hospital ever again.

Twenty yards of linen are worth one coat.

We crossed Yokatopia-dori, and found ourselves in what for the moment was a magical safety zone. I glanced back, but already our hospital, lying beyond the neat, closely packed condo buildings rising above the reclaimed land, was quite invisible. Still to be seen were the metallic blue triangular prism of Fukuoka Tower and the baseball dome with its red-rust-colored roof.

Not far behind me was Nagoyan, pattering along in his sandals. "Let's rest!" he gasped.

He doubled over in the shade of a tree as though about to vomit. We were in a triangular lot overgrown with grass on the north side of an old and superannuated municipal housing development along the river. A sea breeze to which I would normally have been oblivious had bent all of the trees in the direction of the town. We had crossed no more than one boulevard, but suddenly the landscape was subdued, the air thinner.

"I'm out of steam," said Nagoyan by way of excuse.

1

"Hafta stay on the run," I replied, trying to catch my breath. "This is jus' the sorta place we'll get us nabbed."

"On the run? Where to?"

"Doesn't matter – we're on the lam, remember?"

"It's no good! Let's go back."

"A right wuss, aren'tcha Nagoyan!"

He pursed his lips and glared at me.

Twenty yards of linen are worth one coat.

Twenty yards of linen are worth one coat.

We staggered on.

The escape itself wasn't hard. We had been inmates of the Momochi Psychiatric Hospital near Fukuoka Tower, both housed in the open, unisex C Ward. Most of the patients were suffering from depression, but there were also some with symptoms of atypical schizophrenia and psychosis. Momochi is the largest dedicated psychiatric hospital in Kyushu. In addition to C Ward were Wards A, B, D, and E, forming a quadrangular courtyard. A Ward was closed and sex-segregated; B Ward was for drug- and alcohol-dependent patients; Ward D was for children. Ward E was an enigma: rumor had it that those who entered it were never allowed to leave.

Even though we were in a supposedly unrestricted ward, we still called it a prison: Prison C. There were no iron bars, but the windows couldn't be opened wider than three centimeters. Aside from the routine of meals and medication three times a day, there was little for us to do. We had two meetings with the doctor every week, each lasting at most ten minutes.

Having been admitted as manic, I was still very much on an irrepressible high during the initial consultation. I jabbered on and on and then finally asked in high spirits, "Doctor, how much longer till my discharge?"

"You need to stick it out until you've settled down a bit more."

That was all he said. I wasn't allowed any overnights at home, and my parents complied with that, so I came to feel I had no home to return to. My mind remained with the clarity that comes from staying up all night; oddly enough, despite sleep deprivation, I was still physically healthy. The summer was waning, even as I dithered

– dithered as to what to do in this, the one and only summer of my twenty-first year. In my crazed mind, turgid water was surging. It was all so excruciating – the loathsome idea of ending the season there in prison.

The path along the river was largely deserted. Tottering from fatigue, we were headed toward Showa Avenue. The sight of Nishijin Palace's giant bowling pin meant that we were quite close to Nishijin Station – and that is my briar patch. There may not be any luxury items on sale there, but it has almost everything else. Normally, it was fun just to stroll along, looking at the battalion of vendor carts stretching down the middle of the street all the way to Fujisaki, with fresh vegetables and flowers to sell. Fortunately, we were dressed in ordinary clothes; Nagoyan in a polo shirt and chinos, myself in a T-shirt and jeans.

At the hospital, reveille was at six-thirty. At seven we gathered in the dining room and did our NHK radio exercises. We were told that in order to maintain the semblance of normal life, we were to wear everyday attire, not pajamas. We were also forbidden to take naps. The prescribed footwear was sandals, not slippers. We took baths during morning hours on Tuesdays and Fridays; on other days, we were unable even to shower. I wasn't exactly sticky with sweat, as the air conditioning system's thermostat was set so low that it gave me headaches, but having only twice-weekly baths caused me to worry about my armpits and to forgo wearing anything sleeveless.

We were allowed to watch television for only two hours, between five and seven in the evening, with everyone gathered in the dining room. I was suffering from hallucinations and was afraid that they would blend in with the sound of the TV. Between two and five in the afternoon, we were allowed to take up to an hour's walk about the hospital grounds. By entering our names in the sign-out log, we could have a nurse open the door for us. Within the grounds there was really nowhere to go; our options were to stroll to and fro in the well-kept courtyard or walk across the street from the hospital to the local Lawson. Yet undertaking even that modest venture beyond the gate was vastly better than being cooped up in the ward.

Twenty yards of linen are worth one coat.

I had decided that morning to make a run for it. That meant wearing shoes, not sandals. And, of course, I couldn't take anything with me, as a nurse was checking on everyone leaving the ward. In my pockets were my purse and house key.

I had intended to leave alone but changed my mind when I saw Nagoyan. Squatting in a corner of the courtyard, a sad expression on his face, he was playing with a stray cat that scampered off as I approached.

I stood next to Nagoyan and said, "Say, let's make a break fer it."

His response to my suggestion was a puzzled "Huh?"

"Let's *go*! Let's git *out* of 'ere!"

Nagoyan's heart was not really in it, but he toddled along nonetheless.

We passed through the outpatient department, turned toward the rear of the hospital, and exited from the parking lot. As there was not so much as a security guard there, all we had to do to get out without a hitch was not to act in a hurry.

We entered a residential neighborhood. I had already been champing at the bit to the point of explosion, so once we lost sight of the low fence surrounding the hospital, I began to run.

"Hey, Hana-chan! Wait a minute!" shouted Nagoyan, as he followed me.

Nagoyan's real name was Yomogida Tsukasa, a bit of a mouthful, so at first we all carefully called him Yomogida-san. He in turn called me Hanada-san. He was a twenty-four-year-old company man with dyed brown hair.

While everyone else talked in the thick local speech of Hakata, Saga, Chikko, and Kita-Kyushu, Nagoyan stuck to the national standard. As he thus stood out from the rest of us, he was naturally asked his provenance. "Tokyo!" he declared.

"Must be fearsome hard to live there!" was everyone's comment, but he invariably issued a placid denial, "Nothing of the kind... For the moment I happen to be in Kyushu, but eventually I'll be going back."

It was all a lie. When his parents came for their one and only visit, they squawked in pure Nagoya dialect. Those of us who had never been out of Kyushu and had only heard such speech in television dramas were most curious, and so we all, save for an ailing patient who returned to his ward, remained in the dining room, eager to eavesdrop.

"Ya know, Tsukasa," his mother remarked, "Grannie's been awful worried 'bout ya!"

"No sense frettin' on it, now that you've already got yusself put into hospital," said his father.

The entire dining room reverberated with the sound. Our faces were contorted with the strain of suppressed giggles. Nagoyan did not slip once in his use of "proper language," not even with his own parents. I thought them an odd family indeed, with their different ways of talking, but then I suppose the father and mother may well have been wondering whether it was being in a psychiatric hospital that gave people such stifled expressions.

As soon as the two had left, our crowd of idlers circled in on Nagoyan, engulfing him in guffaws. That was when he confessed to being from Nagoya, born and bred. At one point, he had protested in a high-pitched voice that his privacy was being violated, but as no one was in a mood to let him off the hook, he capitulated. Further questioning led him to blurt out that he was born in Meito Ward's Gokuraku, Nagoya's equivalent of the Buddhist Pure Land Paradise. He insisted that Meito was the best area in the entire city, but no one was listening to him. Fukuoka had quite a few odd place names of its own, but nothing quite as blissful as Gokuraku.

"An' yer parents're also from that same blessed place, I s'pose."

"Born there ye were and die there ye will too, no doubt!"

That's how we teased him, so that his nickname almost wound up being Gokuraku. Nagoyan bit his lip in a most endearing way.

He had only spent four years in Tokyo, first as a student at Keio University, and then as an employee of a subsidiary of Nippon Telegraph and Telephone Company. He had hoped to remain in the capital and become a Tokyoite. The irony was that the company had posted him to Fukuoka.

Kyushu people may show deference towards Tokyo, but there are still some who regard Hakata as higher on the scale of things and poke fun at everywhere else. This is primarily a consequence of the local belief that all food outside of Kyushu is by comparison insipid. Hakata folk in particular are gourmands par excellence and talk about food the whole year round.

Even with the bad food served in the hospital, the patients' pride remained unchanged. The only delicacies that came to mind at the mention of Nagoya were pork cutlet in miso paste, fried shrimp, and sweet rice jelly. Kyushu really is unrivaled, but when we suggested all of this to Nagoyan, he bristled and exclaimed impulsively, "But you've forgotten about *nagoyan*! Now *that's* a treat!"

"*Nagoyan*? Now whit would that be?" we shot back.

"The Shikishima Bakery's bean-jam bun variety? You've never heard of it?" he glared at us.

He explained that *nagoyan* consists of steamed sponge cake filled with sweet bean paste infused in egg yolk. We had no idea what he was talking about. Up against the ropes, he flashed back that Shikishima is the most renowned bakery in Nagoya, with a Tokyo branch bearing the name of Pasco.

"Never 'erd of it," we all said, acknowledging his explanation with a willful twist of our own. "Must be summat like our own Ryoyu bread."

Not only had he covered up his roots, but here he was making quite a show of his fondness for Nagoya bean-jam bun – and from a particular bakery no less! There were hoots of laughter, and from then on he was known to everyone but the doctors and nurses as "Nagoyan," the grannie brigade being just reserved enough to call him "Nagoyan-san." Nagoyan heartily loathed the nickname but eventually seemed to resign himself to it.

2

We were already sweating by the time we had made our way to Nishijin, and so we immediately headed for the Purariba department store in the station building just to cool off in its air conditioning. There, not having brought along a towel, I bought a terrycloth handkerchief. I saw that I had only three thousand yen in my purse. Nagoyan was assiduously mopping his brow with his own properly folded hankie. Whether from all our running or from sheer tension, we were both terribly thirsty. I suggested that we get something to drink in Hanajam down on the basement floor; breathing heavily, he nodded. Once we had gulped down the water set on the table before us, I ordered iced tea, while Nagoyan, for some reason, decided on orange juice jelly.

"Come on, take a bite. It's good!"

I took him up on his offer and tasted the slushy stuff, but my mind was somewhere else. What were we to do? What were we to do? Nishijin was indeed something like my own home turf, but that made it dangerous. Someone I knew might see us. My heart was pounding as we quickly left Hanajam and got on the subway. I got the scary feeling that the people sitting across from us were carefully studying our features. Instead of going all the way to Hakata Station, we got off at Tenjin.

"First up, we gotta do some bankin'."

"Why?"

"Escape stash… Better get to it now. Else they'll be on our scent…"

"Scent? What are you talking about?"

"It's like this. If we take out our dough when we're already some way down the road, it's a sure way to tell 'em where we are! Don'tcha get it, Nayoyan? Yer jus' daft, that's what."

He sulked, but when we were again at the street level, he happily called out, "Ah, Tokyo Mitsubishi Bank!" and, crossing the street, headed for the trademark red overlapping circles. "When in Fukuoka…" I wanted to tell him, but with Nagoyan the fact that Fukuoka Bank had branches everywhere was secondary to the pleasure of using a cash card emblazoned with the name of the capital.

At the ATM I took out thirty thousand yen, Nagoyan a lot more. He casually stuffed the thick wad of bills into his pocket and said as soon as we had left the bank, "Let's go back to the hospital after all."

"No way! I'm not goin' back!"

"But that's where we can get cured!"

"If I hafta swallow any more of that Tetropin, I jus' know I'll end up a vegetable. I won't have it!"

If getting cured meant taking that stuff, I'd rather remain ill. The doctor told me it would calm my excitable nerves, a manifestation of my mania and schizophrenia, but it wasn't so simple a matter. All the patients on it say it "curdles" them. It's true. After every dose, you feel just terrible, as though a dark fog had descended over your brain. A paralyzing listlessness sets in that makes it impossible to speak or even to think. You forget whatever you were looking at and lose all track of time. You take it, absent-mindedly pop a sweet into your mouth, and then lose consciousness just like that. When you come to, the goo of the melted candy is still in your mouth. But that isn't to say you've been sleeping. You come to your senses and find that you're itching all over. You scratch the inside of your arms or wherever there's soft skin. And sometimes you get a rash. It's really the pits. To get over it takes at least two hours, and what's scary is that the longer you're on it, the more recovery time you need.

An outpatient might give it a quick toss into the trashcan, but as an inpatient you have to queue up after every meal and before bedtime, cup in hand, with a nurse keeping a watchful eye until you've swallowed it. You can't skip out, stash it, or throw it away. I once had the idea of keeping it under my tongue and spitting it into the toilet, but the nurse caught me. After that, there was an oral inspection to make sure that I had glugged it down.

If I go on being tormented with that Tetropin and wind up unable to return to normal life, I'll be in a total pickle – a real invalid all right. The thought of myself at the end of my days, still confined phantom-like in a hospital, fills me with unbearable dread.

"I won't be goin' back, no matter what! If I take any more o' that Tetropin, I'm done fer. Any more 'n I'll never get back t' normal!"

"Now, now, calm down! It's all right!"

Nagoyan said this with his hands on his hips as we stood in front of the Iwataya department store.

"Tenjin's not safe. Whit'll happen if we're caught?… We hafta go somewhere! What're we t' do, Nagoyan?"

"Don't get excited! Let's just think about it!"

"Awright then…"

"Well," said Nagoyan, with the air of having thrown in the towel, "shall we go to my place?"

Not knowing what to say, I simply nodded. I just wanted to be anywhere that was safe.

We took a train on the Nishitetsu Line. I looked out of the window and saw the Red Cross Hospital in the distance. At Nagoyan's wordless signal, we got off at Takamiya. We walked past the fountain and out to the boulevard, where we caught sight of uniformed middle-school girls from Futaba or Chikushi, apparently on their way home at the end of classes. They all looked so happy. And yet, at their age I too had been the same; in fact, until just recently, I'd been spending my days quite contentedly.

"The Nishitetsu Line's quite sumptin'. All those schools fer proper young ladies."

"So you went straight through state schools?"

"Aye, 'cept fer college."

"Oh! Is Fukuoka University private?"

"'Course it is… I wouldn'a been clever enough fer Kyushu Uni."

Nagoyan's place was in a white-tiled apartment building along a neatly paved road running from the front of the station. When I complimented him on it, he modestly replied that it was only a rental provided by his company.

The only male's room I'd ever known was Tsuyoshi's. He lived with his parents in Sawara Ward. I hadn't seen him in a long time.

Most of the kids I hung around with at college commuted either from the city or from around Kurume. One of my girlfriends came from Isahaya and lived in Ropponmatsu. I often went to visit her in her room. I wondered what had become of her. When I was hospitalized, I underwent a baggage check and had my cell phone taken away and locked up out of reach. Without it, I had no way of knowing anyone's number. So here I was at the ripe old age of twenty-one, venturing for the first time into bachelor quarters.

Nagoyan's one-room flat was austere but tidy. Had he undertaken a massive cleanup prior to his hospitalization? Or was he simply neat by nature? A navy-blue suit wrapped in dry cleaner's plastic was still hanging on a wall hook, which made me marvel at the obvious: that he had previously been going off to a company in appropriately formal attire.

When by Nagoyan's leave I went to the toilet, the seat was up, a reminder of another plain fact: that there was only one person – a male – who had been using the facility. Back in the room, I poked my nose about for a bit, until Nagoya yelled at me to sit down.

In the bay window was a telephone, but, except for my immediate family, the only number I knew off the top of my head was Tsuyoshi's. I thought of calling him but then remembered the icy tone of our last altercation and decided not to. Nagoyan made instant coffee, which we drank with lots of sugar.

"How about some spicy rice crackers?"

"No, ta."

I didn't know why anyone would have rice crackers with coffee, but then Nagoyan said he wouldn't have any either. As he spoke, I sensed that I was still on edge.

Twenty yards of linen are worth one coat.

"I say we wait until you've calmed down a bit and then go back to the hospital. All right?"

"I'll not be goin' back. I'm gonna keep on runnin'."

"That's no good. Come on. Be reasonable!"

Twenty yards of linen are worth one coat.

There was no way I was going to be reasonable.

"Yer sayin' ye don't care if I die?"

"Manic people don't wind up dead."

"Ah, but they do, they do! It's jus' that ye've no idea!"

The more I talked, the more tense and agitated I became, and I began to shake. I could feel the blood vessels in my head pounding wildly.

Twenty yards of linen are worth one coat.

"What do you want me to do?" shouted Nagoyan.

"I'm *tellin'* yer! There's no sayin' what I'll do if you leave me alone."

"So what should we do?"

Twenty yards of linen are worth one coat.

I lowered my voice.

"Th' hospital's bound t' be out lookin' fer us already."

"Yes, indeed. And we're sure to come in for it!"

"They'll 'ave us put into private rooms, wit' barred windows."

We referred quite routinely to rooms locked from the outside as "private." We even joked that there was no extra charge for such accommodations.

"There's one where the only window looks out on the corridor, across from the nurse station. Now that's a place I wouldn't like one bit!"

"An' that's why we gotta keep on runnin'!"

Twenty yards of linen are worth one coat.

Twenty yards of linen are worth one coat.

Twenty yards of linen are worth one coat.

I was already on the verge of tears, not understanding why I was being tormented by that voice. I had a constant sense of unease, as though instead of a hat, I were wearing a wok on my head, with someone banging on it. The one ounce of sanity I still had was urging escape, though I wasn't entirely sure that even that portion of my brain was still in order. At the same time, I was also aware that at any moment someone from the hospital might be ringing the bell. (*We mustn't be here. We must find a place where nobody knows us. Now! Now!*) I had the feeling of being driven by some invisible being.

"Nagoyan, ye've got a car, haven't ye?"

"Yes..."

"Let's make a bolt fer it together. We got no choice."

"I'll take you as far as home, then return the car and go back to the hospital."

"No way!"

"Don't talk like a child!"

But when I stared hard at him, he lowered his eyes. For some time he sat cross-legged, his hands on his knees, but finally he sighed deeply and said, "Really make a clean break of it?"

"Really…"

"I suppose there's no other way."

Assuming that Nagoyan had now made up his mind, I disclosed a concern of mine.

"I got no medicine."

"Would you like to see mine?"

Nagoyan opened a closet and took down a shoebox from the top shelf. It was filled with various drugs.

"If you took the lot of it, would you be dead?" he asked in a silly tone.

"No way ye can kill yerself even with all that! Anyway, there's not the right sort 'ere."

"Oh, now really?"

What I needed a lot more than that sort of scary talk was some effective medicine.

"Have ye got any levomepromazine?"

"I've never heard of it."

"It's got, ye know, Hirunamin. All the same stuff."

"Oh, the sleeping aid."

"What else d'ye take?"

"Rohypnol."

"I need some too. Gotta lot?"

"One sheet's worth."

The rest he had weren't the kind that would work for me. Nagoyan was already a pretty pathetic character, and even the drugs he had weren't up to snuff. I was now strongly on the manic side, so I didn't need any antidepressants, but I still wanted some Limas.

I also wanted to get hold of some Mellaril. Without it, I'd have no way to cope when my hallucinations came on, the visual variety being immeasurably more frightening than the auditory. All sorts of people, multitudes of people, would gather inside me, sleeping or rising as they wished, regardless of my own state – weeping, raging, despairing. The conclusion was always the same: they would all try to kill me. I would tell myself that it was just a delusion, but my voice was so faint as to be drowned out. The delusory had a greater sense of reality, so that the real and the unreal became indistinguishable. I couldn't help worrying that I would spew out whatever the hallucinatory voices were saying. It was all quite absurd.

"Haven't you got any medicine at your parents' house?" asked Nagoyan, as he stuffed his own into a checkout bag.

"I had some awright, but after my attempt, th' lot of it was thrown away."

"You really 'attempted' it?" he said in a stunned whisper.

Yes, I really had attempted it.

I had been in outpatient treatment for depression as a high school girl and had had no idea that I'd flipped over to manic. Having gone through a year and a half without getting horribly down, I had assumed that I was cured. I'd go to the hospital once a month to pick up my medicine, but I only took the barbiturates and put aside the rest. Basically, I'm not the gloomy sort.

I had no reason to try to kill myself, and that's what makes manic suicide so terrifying. At the time, there wasn't a day I didn't enjoy. I went swimming with friends along the beaches of Itoshima Peninsula, drank a lot, blew the money I earned from my part-time job on clothes and cosmetics, and snogged — and occasionally also fought — with my then boyfriend Tsuyoshi, who described me as "high strung." But I was on such a roll that it never occurred to me that this was a symptom of my illness. I think I must have had a jolly good time of it, but now my memory is quite blurred.

I can't remember any of it.

Suddenly, I had a day that was a total blank. It was the first time I heard the voice.

Twenty yards of linen are worth one coat.

Twenty yards of linen are worth one coat.

It was a deep male voice. At first I thought it came from the radio. Sometimes there was static mixed in, but, in fact, I didn't have any radio turned on — except for a broken one in my head.

Twenty yards of linen are worth one coat.

"Today is the day," I said to myself, "that I'm going to die."

The idea was as terribly matter-of-fact as if I'd thought of going off on a jaunt to the Canal City entertainment complex, as though in a flash everything had been laid open before my eyes.

At a convenience store I bought two liters of water and then started downing all of the medicine I'd been hoarding. I knew that the sleeping medicine they give out these days alone wouldn't do the trick. The Vegetamin A that I was taking contained phenobarbital, but only a small amount. I wondered whether lithium carbonate would work. I didn't know what a lethal dose might be. And I'm not sure exactly what I took or in what amounts, but eventually I lost consciousness.

When I awoke, I found myself bound hand and foot to the four corners of a bed in a hospital ward. I couldn't immediately remember what had happened. I felt something rough and stiff in my groin and realized that I was wearing nappies. I had also been equipped with a drip feed and a nasal tube. I had that the feeling that my nose and throat were clogged up.

Well now, ye've got yerself into quite some pickle, I thought.

My father was sitting beside the bed, a ferocious look on his face. "Havin' a tough time of it then, with yer stomach pumped 'n all?" he asked, his expression unchanging.

"Don't remember."

He fell silent again.

"How long was I out?"

"Two days."

"Where is it then, this place?"

"The Red Cross Hospital. In Hirao."

"I hafta make a phone call."

I had immediately thought of Tsuyoshi.

When the nurse arrived, my father went out of the room. She removed the nasal tube and freed my arms and legs. When I asked her whether I'd been that out of control, she nodded with an embarrassed laugh. Then, to my far greater shame, she took off my nappies and cleaned up for me. I was then allowed to go to the toilet by myself, rolling the drip feed apparatus along as I went.

I had badgered my father into getting my cell phone back and then used it to call Tsuyoshi from the toilet. I apologized to him for not having been in touch, but it seemed that my mother had already told him what had happened. Even though I knew I was in the wrong, I couldn't help feeling resentment toward her.

Tsuyoshi was silent for a moment, then said, "I'd no idea ye were mental."

There was a harsh tone in his voice that I had never heard before. "What? It's got nothin' to do wit' us or anythin'!"

"Ye've fankled me jus' fine!" he muttered, whatever that meant. I knew it wasn't anything nice.

"No!" I shouted frantically.

"Anyway, it's over. I don't care fer ye." I heard the phone click.

After that, my calls to him were blocked. Hoping that he would have a change of heart and end hostilities, I kept trying to get through, and when that didn't work, I called his home, only to be told that he was out. Not wanting to be taken for a stalker, I finally gave up, as much as that hurt. But I still loved him.

Tsuyoshi had reached adulthood without growing out of that king-of-the-little-ruffians mode. He was dark complexioned and seemed to be a bit of a noodle, but, in fact, he was a terribly lonely bloke who sulked whenever I went off to have fun with other friends. He was awfully kind and gentle, so that I somehow assumed he would protect me from whatever grim encounters life might bring. When I was with him, I also became more fond of myself. I loved him simply because he loved me.

But that was all over now.

My only salvation was the timing, as first-term exams were already behind me. My state of frenzy continued. I easily became emotional, flying into rages and kicking the wall. I couldn't concentrate, read, or get a good night's sleep. My parents were trying to keep me cooped up in the house, and I quarreled constantly with them. It was particularly hard, as the confinement only made my rampages worse. They themselves didn't understand the nature of my illness. I would tell them that if they didn't believe me, they could ask the doctors, but when they met them for consultation, all they said was "yes, Doctor, yes," without comprehending a word that was being said.

I once escaped by squeezing through a ground-level dust outlet, realizing only too late that I was in what had become my nightwear: high-school PE clothes and a tattered T-shirt. Thus attired, wearing my father's flip-flops, I made my way in great embarrassment to Tenjin, where, without realizing what I was doing, I bought this and that and wound up with shopping bags in both hands: a stuffed animal, sandals, eating utensils… My fretfulness and compulsiveness had become too much even for me.

In the meantime, the paperwork for my admission to Momochi Hospital had been done. I put up no resistance. I thought at the time that having committed the grave crime of attempted suicide, I had no choice.

Twenty yards of linen are worth one coat.

3

Nagoyan packed his medicine into his rucksack, rolled up T-shirts and pairs of jeans, stuffed them in, and then went to the bathroom cabinet to retrieve his hair wax and electric shaver. It did indeed seem that we were setting out on a journey. Seeing that his carefully folded underwear consisted of boxer shorts, I felt strangely relieved, even though it obviously had nothing to do with me. I was worried about what to do myself in that department, but was much too ashamed to say so.

"Would ye lend me a couple of T-shirts?" I asked.

"Sure," he replied and tossed in two more. They were of a grayish color.

From the standpoint of time alone, it would be much too hazardous to go pick up anything from home. Besides, I had not the slightest excuse for showing up there. My parents would probably not allow it and might have already been tipped off by a call from the hospital.

There was a parking lot in the residential street behind the apartment building. Nagoyan's car was an old, rectangular geezer crate – and white to boot. It didn't fit the image of a stylish young man with dyed brown hair.

"A Nagoya license plate…" I sniggered, having never seen one before on the road.

"Don't laugh," he said. "One of these days I'll be sporting Shinagawa plates."

The thought of upmarket Tokyo plates on that car was a crackup. Shinagawa, indeed.

"It's jus' like a scene from *Howling at the Sun*."

I had remembered an episode with the macaroni cop and the Boss."

"What do you mean?"

"There's a corpse in the trunk, 'n at th' end, the car explodes 'n burns."

"Huh?"

Nagoyan smiled wryly and heaved his rucksack into his corpseless trunk. For an instant, as I got in on the passenger's side, I smelled the faint odor of an unknown male. Somehow I found my heart pounding. Though I had no particular interest in the answer, I asked him, "Whit's the make o' this car?"

"It's a Luce. My father gave it to me when he bought a new one."

I grunted some sort of reply, to which Nagoyan added, "Even so, it's been called the 'Hiroshima Mercedes'."

I couldn't understand what the boast was all about. Would people refer to the Hiroshima Baseball Stadium as "Hiroshima's Fukuoka Dome"?

Nagoyan started the engine. The sound of punk rock emerged from a cassette tape, the car being too old for a CD player.

"Whit's the group?" I asked.

"The Peas. Not Going Back Anywhere."

He rewound the tape.

My brains are in the way,
Half of 'em will do.
I just don't want to get involved...
My brains are in the way.

The message seemed so "to the moment" as to have been contrived.

"They got back together a few years ago."

"Huh? Is this whit ye like then?"

"Do you, Hana-chan?"

"It's awright."

I hadn't expected this. I would have thought him to be one for quieter music.

The road that led to Route 3 was congested; Nagoyan was clearly irritated.

Twenty yards of linen are worth one coat.

When a car in the next lane forced its way into ours, he screeched, "These crazy drivers!! You can blink your turn signal till you're blue in the face and they still won't let you in. And then they bulldoze their way into *your* lane as if they wanted to mow you down! It's really only the Fukuokans who get to me. In Tokyo, we've got gentlemen behind the wheel!"

"Why dont'cha jus' give 'em a loud honk?"

"Why is it that even girls like you talk such rot? The point is that it's a matter of manners, isn't it?"

"If ye want t' survive on the road 'round here, ye hafta show some guts."

I remembered what a hot-blooded driver Tsuyoshi was. He'd roll down the window and scream. Here, even the buses careen about. My father would always carry a wooden sword in the trunk of his car, which is why Nagoyan's raging about it all was so absurd. Once you're out on the public road, you never know when you'll run into someone who's hauling around a thing like that. It's really that dicey. ...Not that I was a driver myself.

"Are we really going to do this? I can't help thinking that it's a bad idea after all. In fact, I get the feeling that it's *quite* a bad idea."

Nagoyan kept talking like that, but I said nothing. Having been thinking that we were on a journey to a place far, far away, I realized that we were now on the old Route 3. There was something nostalgic about the dreary landscape.

I bade a silent farewell to my native Fukuoka.

"Where should we be heading?"

"Haven't ye got a navi?"

"How could I? This is a 1987 car. If you want a map, you'll find one in the glove compartment."

"1987? Now that's, like, *old!*"

In the glove compartment was a map of Fukuoka's byways, along with one of the twenty-three wards of Tokyo and yet another – the kind provided in service areas – of the entire Kyushu expressway system. That was it. *Not very promising*, I thought. I opened up the expressway map, but nothing in it could tell me where to go. Even with a navigator, I would have been no less clueless.

Twenty yards of linen are worth one coat.

"Say, Hana-chan, wouldn't it be better to go back? This is going to get awfully sticky."

Nagoyan had only called my name when he was in a bind, when, for example, he was feeling too down even to go to the hospital kiosk and wanted me to buy him some juice. But now his car was headed down the road, with music blaring. The weather was perfect, and if I hadn't had that voice in my ear, it would have been a marvelous day.

Nagoyan didn't need to look so grim; after all, I was the only one being tormented by "Twenty yards…" But I suppose his bad moods were an unavoidable consequence of his depression.

"Say, where do you live?"

"There," I replied, pointing in the direction of Kasugabaru.

"Stop talking nonsense."

Nagoyan was no fool. It was clearly not the way to Jonan Ward.

"All right. Which way is Aso?"

The sudden question surprised me.

"Um. Ower there. South."

"It's a famous spot for suicides, isn't it?"

"Why're ye sayin' that? It's a good place. I wouldna mind goin' there now!"

"No! You've got to go home!"

"Nagoyan," I remarked with a smirk, "how'd it be if ye were to go back to Gokuraku?"

At this, he suddenly sat up straight, declaring, "I'm never going to go back to Nagoya! That was the whole point of my studying to get into a university in Tokyo."

"Must be terribly sad fer a Keio boy t' find himself stuck in Kyushu – even if it is such a grand place!"

Nagoyan bit his lip.

"I'm going back someday to Tokyo – for sure!" he exclaimed, quite as though he were taking an oath of vengeance.

"Well, shall we be goin' there then?"

Tokyo was all about a fun-filled visit. It wasn't a place you'd want to live in.

"By car? No way!"

Nagoyan would bite his lip when vexed or frustrated. As he himself was aware, it gave him quite a loveable look, so that when he was really at the end of his wits, I knew so immediately from the way he would throw back his head and narrow his eyes. He was rather good-looking but his face tended to be divided between upper and lower portions, so that when he forced a smile, it was only with his mouth. When he was feeling pleased with himself, he would raise his eyebrows. And when he was annoyed, his eyes and nose would go off in their own directions, as though a game of pin-the-features-on-the-face were being played. To know his true emotions, I had to observe the upper portion; what he wanted people to see was revealed in the lower portion. I wasn't very good at explaining it all to him, and when I did, he exclaimed, "Please don't be *scrutinizing* me!" Still, as I could see from the shy smile on the upper half of his face, he was pleased at being poked and prodded in this way.

"Shall we take the expressway?"

Twenty yards of linen are worth one coat.

Twenty yards of linen are worth one coat.

"No way! They'll be on the lookout fer us there!"

I really thought so. I was sure of it.

"Come on! You're getting paranoid."

"They're bound t' be checkin' the bullet train and th' expressways. The highways are th' only roads that're safe."

"What shall we do then? Turn back?"

Nagoyan's eyes narrowed, a sign that he was frightened.

"Gettin' caught means bein' put in private rooms."

"Then how about this...?"

Nagoyan flipped the turn signal and took Route 386. I didn't know where we were heading, but this had clearly been a fork in the road.

4

———

"My dream was to save up money and buy a Porsche. A Boxter."

I didn't know what he was talking about.

"Huh?"

"Don't you know what a Porsche is? It's a German car."

"No. I ain't even got a license."

"You're joking! You were a college student, weren't you?"

"Nagoyan, are ye some sorta car nerd?"

"I don't think so, but a Porsche-less world is for me unimaginable."

"Yer bloody loony to be findin' that so 'unimaginable' when y'aint even got one!"

"Don't call me loony!"

"Nagoyan, how much cash did ye get from the bank?"

It was a question that had been on my mind for some time, but Nagoyan answered with nonchalance, "A million yen."

"*What?*"

"It doesn't matter. A hundred thousand, a million... It's all the same."

I thought I saw some roadside fruit stands. Amagi was the first real community we'd seen since leaving Fukuoka City. But it was small.

"We need to eat something."

"Already?"

"Oh, but I just remembered. You're never hungry, are you?"

In the hospital, I would always leave food uneaten. About the only thing I could eat was yogurt. Even I thought it strange that I had no appetite. In my manic phase, I didn't sleep, I didn't eat, and I didn't tire. And so I shrank.

"I dunno if it was because o' my illness or because o' the food."

"I had thought that the bad image of 'hospital food' was just that, an image, and that recently it had improved, but it really was horrible, wasn't it?"

"A hundered times worse than school-caf fare."

"Tuesday's 'noodle day' was really the pits, wasn't it? Wheat-flour, buckwheat, whatever... It would suck up the liquid, so there was no broth left."

"And that chicken sauté was really dreadful! It stank like a chicken coop. It was so oily that I couldna finish it."

Nagoyan pulled the car in at an outlet of the Hamakatsu chain restaurant. Inured as we were to barnyard feed, it seemed a shame simply to gobble up the piping hot, scrumptious pork cutlet. Even the miso soup had the taste of real stock, unlike anything we had had in the hospital. It occurred to me that I had quite a healthy appetite when the food was good and I could truly enjoy the taste. I had a second helping of the glistening white rice. Nagoyan too was eating like a horse. All through the meal, until our coffee arrived, we exchanged not a word. For the first time in a long while, a sense of satisfaction was permeating my entire being. I felt like a ruminating cow.

"Since we've come this far," I suggested, "let's go on to Akizuki!"

"What is there to see there?"

Akizuki was where Tsuyoshi and I had our last date. I needed to wipe Tsuyoshi from my mind like chalk from a blackboard, but that wasn't why we had made our escape, so I merely said, "Nothin' really... I jus' wanna go there."

I had absolutely no desire to go by myself, but I had the feeling that unless I went, taking someone else along, I'd never be able to manage it again. There was really nothing there, but I loved its quiet, intimate atmosphere and didn't want to give it all up.

The area was already enveloped in the twilight as we arrived. I said I wanted to walk through the cherry trees in Suginobaba. Though the foliage was darkly luxuriant, there was something both sad and nostalgic about the dried-up moat. A middle school had been built on the castle ruins. The buildings had a rather dapper appearance, in Japanese style.

Gazing at the facility, I remarked to Nagoyan, "Ye'd 'ave memories for a lifetime if ye'd gone to a school like this."

"I have no memories of my time in middle school," he rebuffed me.

We climbed the magnificent stone steps just across the way to a small, ancient shrine. I prayed that I might recover from my illness –

and that we might not be caught. Nagoyan was long at his own prayers, no doubt beseeching the gods to make him a Tokyoite or to put him in a Porsche.

I thought that by this time the hospital might already be in an uproar. Would my parents be scurrying about to find me? If a missing persons search request were issued, would the police be set in motion too? Were we now really in some sort of *Howling at the Sun* episode? Would there be a mushrooming slew of cop cars on the chase, with us being cornered at the end of some wharf, Nagoyan brandishing a knife as he held me hostage, the police coaxing him over a loudspeaker to give himself up and his mother finally coming out in tears and falling in dejection at our knees?

It was all quite inconceivable. Here it was so peaceful.

"They've surely gone to Itoshima!"

"What?"

"I love the sea, ye know, so they're sure t' go lookin' fer us in Itoshima and Kanesaki."

"Uh-huh," he replied listlessly.

"I've always wanted to see Hirado."

"Hirado… That's in Nagasaki, right?"

"Uh-huh. An' here they won't be lookin' fer us right away."

"I wonder… What lies down the road from here?"

"Beppu, I s'pose. Then maybe Yufuin, and then to the south, Aso."

"So we wind up in Aso after all."

"Haven't ye been there?"

To my amazement, it turned out that Nagoyan had not been to any of the fun places in Kyushu.

"What did ye *do* on holidays?"

"I usually slept. For Golden Week, I'd go to Tokyo."

Aw, Tokyo again, I thought wearily.

On the way back from Akizuki to Amaki, I suddenly felt a chill. Going only on intuition, I told Nagoyan that we should turn left. I somehow wanted to get away from highways and towns, even if only for a short distance. The way would presumably take us toward the village of Koishiwara. Dusk fell as we found ourselves following a pitch-black mountain road.

"Shimada-san must be fuming. I suppose she'll be worried about me."

Shimada-san was a pretty nurse in Ward C who would be turning twenty-seven; she was three years older than Nagoyan. I had no way of knowing, but I thought that she might have a boyfriend.

"Ye like 'er then, do ye, Nagoyan?"

"I wouldn't say I have a crush on her or anything, but I suppose she's my type."

"No, really? She jus' loves to give enemas!"

The side effects of the medicine, inexperience with old-fashioned squat toilets, and lack of exercise meant that many patients were constipated. After three days without relief, enemas were the prescribed procedure. In a sweet voice, Nurse Shimada would smilingly say to me, "If you've still had no luck today..."

The frightening mental image of it was indelible.

"It's not that she enjoys doing it. It's just part of her job."

"Whenever she had me in 'er clutches, she seemed giddy with it all, before and after. Her eyes'd sparkle."

"Really?"

"Sure. I suppose ye'd be delighted to be back in hospital, havin' it dun to ye by yer beloved Shimada."

"How can you talk like that?" he huffed. "Don't go spoiling my image of her!"

We parked the car in the remotest corner of the Koishiwara rest area parking lot.

"This is it for the day."

"What? We're gonna sleep in the car?"

"What else can we do?"

We downed our sleeping medicine with the help of the Volvic mineral water we had bought at the convenience store. Nagoyan then took out a cigarette from his rucksack and lit it. It was a Salem Light.

"Do ye smoke, Nagoyan? I'd no idea."

"Just one before bedtime. It works magic."

I had him give me one. I choked on the fumes.

In the darkness, with the engine turned off, I was, as one might well expect, a bit frightened. I was on friendly terms with Nagoyan, but he was nonetheless an unrelated male. Fortunately, there was no auditory hallucination. We had leaned the seats back and were resting next to each other. I told myself that once the medicine kicked in, it wouldn't matter where I was and that it would soon be morning. I couldn't see Nagoyan, but sensed that he too was wide awake.

"Ten thirty, eh?" he muttered.

"It were always lights out at nine."

"Everybody must be asleep by now."

"Wonder whit they're sayin' 'bout our escape."

"Stop it. No use thinking about it now."

I hated the silence. Neither he nor I nor anyone else knew why we were here in such a place.

"Nagoyan, tomorrow ye need to teach me t' drive."

"No way, absolutely no way!"

"If ye do all the drivin', ye'll wear yerself out."

"You've said yourself you don't have a license"

"But if they catch us, aw they'll do is send us back to hospital. We jus' need to lie low here in the countryside. I'll be able t' manage."

In low voices we talked a bit more and then fell asleep.

I woke up as it was starting to get light, about three, and couldn't doze off again. It was bright and chilly outside. I went to the toilet, bought a can of coffee, and returned to the car. After that and until Nagoyan woke up, I heard the voice saying over and over again:

Twenty yards of linen are worth one coat.

Twenty yards of linen are worth one coat.

Twenty yards of linen are worth one coat.

I had the unbearable and terrifying sensation of my hijacked brain starting to go on the rampage. The sight and sound of Nagoyan's peaceful slumber filled me with spite.

5

Even though the idea of learning to drive had been mine, I felt extremely nervous. Nagoyan proved to be a good instructor.

"All right. You put your right foot on the foot brake and use your left hand to lower the hand brake. Fine. Now with your left foot on the clutch, shift to first gear. Yes, you've got it. Look back over your right shoulder. Uh-huh. Now move your right foot to the gas pedal and slowly push down, as you also gradually let up on the clutch. Yes. The clutch is on the left. Okay. A bit more pressure on the gas pedal. Get ready to put your foot on the clutch again. Oh, you don't need to brake. Push the clutch all the way down and shift to second gear. Now turn the steering wheel slightly to the right. Good…"

There in the deserted rest area parking lot, I practiced starting the engine, shifting gears, and turning left and right, before moving out onto the road. Nagoyan was long-suffering: no matter how often I let the engine die or turned too sharply, he never chewed me out. He merely gave me immediate pointers.

"When you're going around a curve, keep your eye on where you come out of it. That way your hands will automatically turn the steering wheel in the right direction."

"The first time you hit the brakes is to send a signal to the car behind you; the second time is to see that they're working; the third time is to stop."

"It's hard to get the hang of it at first, but you need to make constant use of the side-view and rear-view mirrors. Not staring into them, but rather keeping your eyes moving about."

It was a narrow country road, so whenever Nagoyan told me that a car was approaching from the rear, I would flip the turn signal and pull over to the left to let it pass. I initially drove at barely thirty kilometers per hour but was gradually able to get up to forty.

"The idea of having you drive was to let me get some rest. But you're keeping me rather busy!" Nagoyan said with a laugh. "Let's take a break."

He had me pull into a convenience store parking lot. I stalled the car twice before finally managing to back up and park outside the entrance.

Seeing me shuffling about inside, Nagoyan said he would take a nap in the car. I hastily bought underwear for a hefty seven hundred yen, went to the restroom, and changed into it. The pair I had been wearing was still warm in my hand from my body heat. Hesitating for a moment, I finally pushed them into the sanitary napkin disposal bin.

We drove by a vineyard. Without thinking, I braked. The car behind us honked. Nagoyan and I exchanged glances and the next moment had gotten out of the car and slipped our way in. We broke off clumps of grapes one after another, popped the watery globules into our mouths, and savored the sweetness of stolen fruit. And now it was impossible for us to stop ourselves. Next came a field of tomatoes and then a field of cucumbers. The vines were surprisingly tough, and tearing at them with our hands was no easy task.

"If we had barbeque equipment, we could have quite a feast with eggplant or corn," said Nagoyan, munching on a cucumber, quite oblivious to the right or wrong of it all.

We crossed a minor mountain pass and went loping along until the road began to wind through the Yabakei Gorge. Here I had been as a child on a family outing. As I saw through the windshield the sluggishly hovering dragonflies, I remembered chasing and catching them in the riverbed.

"I've been meanin' t' ask ye why ye don't speak your native dialect."

"Don't you know 'The limits of my language are the limits of my world'? I don't want my world to be limited by Nagoya."

"Whit is that supposed t' mean?"

"It's been common sense ever since Wittgenstein."

"An' who'd that be?"

"He's said to be the last philosopher. He came up with the idea that philosophy is the same as the language game. It would behoove you to know that sort of thing."

Whenever Nagoyan embarked on an irksome topic, the wings of his nose would quiver with pleasure. Even when I didn't understand very well what he was talking about, it was so much fun to watch him that even when were in the hospital, I'd pose all sorts of questions.

"'Whereof one cannot speak, thereof one must be silent.' That's a famous saying of his."

Again I didn't understand, so I deliberately made an irrelevant remark. "How d'ye say *soiginta* in Nagoya dialect?"

Soiginta is what you say to someone who is leaving, but it's actually Saga dialect, so I don't happen to use it myself.

"I don't know what it means. I never use any kind of local speech."

"Well, now if that don't take the cake!"

"I don't talk like that. I really don't."

As he spouted his pointless argument, I imagined a huge column of mosquitoes swirling inside his head. If magnified, they would number in the millions, buzzing about and all having the same twangy sound of Nagoyan's relatives and fellow locals. Such an idea wouldn't have occurred to that Wittgen-whatever-his-name-was. As I envisaged Nagoyan waving his hands about as he weepingly fought off the mosquito host, I found myself suppressing a laugh. Nagoyan gave me a puzzled look.

"It's nothin'. It's jus' that I would'a thought it a good thing to be able t' speak the local talk."

"You should learn to talk properly."

"I can, but I don't."

"Why? That's crazy!"

"It's the blood o' Kyushu that runs in me veins. I'm proud of it, 'n of me language too."

"Nowadays all that talk about 'blood' is so *old*!"

"But what of yer lyin' that ye were born in Tokyo?"

"I didn't lie. Because it *is* true that I went from Tokyo to Fukuoka."

"Why'd ye want t' cover up where ye were born? Now, *that's* crazy!"

"You can only say that because you weren't born in Nagoya. If you had been, you'd understand."

Nagoyan would speak in a high-pitched voice whenever the subject of Nagoya came up. It was odd, because people normally spoke softly on matters they wished to conceal.

"Understand what?"

"My complexes. Nagoyans are like a walled city, the way Japan was when it cut itself off from the rest of the world. And the clingy sound of the dialect is simply unbearable. Yes, my parents speak it, but from the time I was small, I was determined not to. I wanted to leave home as quickly as I could. Besides, Tokyoites look down their noses at Nagoyans."

I don't know what Tokyoites do, but it seemed to me that Nagoyan would feel picked on no matter where he went. Because the slightest bit of teasing was all it took to produce on his face the sort of "feel-good pain" you get from a good massage. It made you want to go on goading him. Though he would never admit it, he was a classic case of masochism.

"But, you know," he exclaimed with a sense of relief, "if we were in a Porsche now, we'd stick out like a sore thumb."

"We'd be caught fer sure, awright. Jus' as well we're in this scrapheap!"

"I like it here, this ravine. I like streams better than the ocean anyway."

"Oh? But it's hardly anythin' out o' th' ordinary."

It occurred to me that scenery the likes of Yabakei Ravine can be seen all over Kyushu. I had nothing against it, of course, but if it is true that the poet-philosopher Rai San'yo was so overwhelmed at the sight that he broke his brush in two and threw in the towel, so to speak, all I can say is that he wasn't all that well informed.

As we drove, we passed a tourist advertisement bearing the likeness of the statesman Yukichi Fukuzawa and informing us that the Memorial Hall erected to him lay straight ahead.

"Why here?" exclaimed Nagoyan.

"Ye mean the bloke on the ten thousand yen ticket? He came from Nakatsu."

"You should at least be able to refer to it as the ten thousand yen *banknote*."

"Ten thousand yen ticket" was what Tsuyoshi called it, and at some point I'd picked up the expression.

"You know, I went to Keio University for four years and never knew that our founder was from Kyushu."

"He's th' one who said 'heaven bestows only a single blessing,' right?"

"No, no. He said, 'Heaven does not make one man higher – or lower – than another.'"

"So everyone at Keio's quite fond of 'im?"

"I wouldn't say 'fond'. He's thought of as a great man... Since we've come this far anyway, let's have a look."

Nagoyan talked about a book by Fukuzawa, written for the education of children, in which the beloved old folk tale of Momotaro is criticized as a tale of aggressive warfare waged against "ogres" who, though innocent of any wrongdoing, suffer the invasion of their island and the theft of their treasure. I was willing to go along with that, but I still didn't know whether Fukuzawa was a great man.

The area through which the road to Nakatsu passed was well developed, but we seemed to see nothing but funeral halls and shops selling household altars, one after another. I wondered how with so few people living here, there could be so many people dying.

"Creepy!" exclaimed Nagoyan.

Yukichi Fukuzawa's childhood home was a dilapidated, straw-thatched house. I was bored by the Memorial Hall, but Nagoyan seemed more than satisfied, as he excitedly pointed to the aerial photographs, "Look! There's the Mita campus, and here's the Hiyoshi campus! Ah, those were the days!"

"Yukichi," we read, "bade farewell to Nakatsu in buoyant spirits." It occurred to me that Nagoyan might well have left Nagoya in much the same frame of mind.

Next to the Memorial Hall was a modest café. We stood outside, looking at the lunch menu.

"Wonder what the Yukichi lunch is?"

"Deep-fried, soy-flavored chicken, it says."

"How can they call such cheap fare the 'Yukichi lunch'?"

He seemed genuinely indignant. I burst out laughing.

"Deep-fried sounds awright to me. I'd wager it's quite tasty."

"No... In Oita, there'll be more variety. Bungo beef steak or branded horse mackerel... If one is going to put Yukichi's name to food..."

"S'pose it'd haf to be a dinner costin' a full Fukuzawa ticket, wouldn't it now?"

Nagoyan turned on his heel and huffily returned to the car.

In the end, we stopped again at the highway rest area, where in the restaurant there I made quite a show of ordering and eating a set meal of deep-fried, soy-flavored chicken. It seemed to be the culinary pride of Nakatsu, after all.

The evening cicadas were whining. I felt as though my ribs were being squeezed. There was no place to which we might return. We would be stopping here for the night, with nothing to do but sleep in the car.

I had imagined a still and quiet night, but suddenly from the area loudspeakers blared the melody of *Back Home*.

"Hey! Lay off!" Nagoyan shouted.

"What time is it?"

"Nine."

"Time fer sleep, isn't it?"

"Huh? We're not in the hospital!"

I had always thought it ridiculous that it was lights out at nine, saying that I liked to stay up late, but here we were keeping to that same absurd schedule ourselves.

"Ah, that startled me!"

We took our medicine and smoked a Salem Light.

The barbiturates didn't work. I was usually an easy sleeper, despite being afflicted with early morning awakening, so now that I was wide awake, my foremost thoughts were of our weird, abnormal behavior – and of the wrong we had done. Had we been right to run away? Would we be caught? Waves of sleep were rolling back and forth with the lithe motion of a broom, catching only Nagoyan in their embrace, taking him away and leaving me behind as debris. Would I be taken back to the hospital, put away in a private room, with Tetropin piled mountain high, and left to congeal? Terrified by such thoughts, I would fretfully wake, sometimes going to the women's room or walking around the rest area. Just when I thought I'd fallen asleep at last, the din of *Back Home* came on again. It was six o'clock. Nagoyan appeared to have already awoken some time before.

6

Passing through Usa-hachiman, we left Route 10 and came to Kunisaki Peninsula. The scenery abruptly shifted. What hills there were could not be called mountains. It was as though we were surrounded by rough mounds of soft clay that had been slapped together and stuck at oblique angles to each other. Was it the hills that were at a tilt or was it the flat terrain? My nerves were set on edge by the feeling that sky and earth had turned to contorted mush.

"Aren't ye afraid?"

Nagoyan, slack-jawed, replied with a nod. He reminded me of a dog whose tail has steadily drooped and is on the verge of dropping between its hind legs.

"This would be a scary place if there were somehow, you know, a haunting presence…"

"Oh, but there *is*."

Nagoyan let out a shriek.

"They're here, they're here! Lots of 'em. I can see one gettin' on yer shoulder now. An' another!"

"Eeeek!" Nagoyan screeched again, convulsing like a wild beast, as he sought to shake off the unseen spirits.

"No, no, ye don' get it!"

"What?"

"I 'ave delusions awright, but I don' see ghosts."

"You're certainly a laid-back one! A person of my sensitivity can't take this."

As "laid-back" as I might be, the eeriness of our surroundings was clear to me as well.

"Don'tcha worry. Let's go somewhere ordinary and normal."

We had quite lost our bearings, but by following the tourist signs we made our way to Fukidera. I was in the mood to show off this temple, which is the finest that I know. Though famous, it stands there amidst the stillness of the hills as it has for ages, with nothing the least bit worldly about it, blending in perfectly with the wildflowers. The main hall's distinguishing feature was an elegant roof with upturned flaring corners, which seen from above must have appeared square. The smell of incense in the dark interior was likewise refined, lending a sense of tranquility.

"A gentle-looking Buddha, isn't he now?" I remarked.

"I think it's the Tendai sect… The Tendai sect is, um…"

Nagoyan started to make a comment, then, having seemed to have lost his train of thought, said that one should look at the statue in a sitting rather than a standing position, so that one's upward gaze perfectly meets the half-closed eyes of the Buddha.

The disturbed state of mind in which I had found myself just a short time ago was quite gone. We entered the tearoom across the way from the temple.

"What'll we eat?"

"Dumplings with miso. That's th' normal fare 'ere."

"What is it like?"

"Vegetables and dumplings in miso broth."

I had a great fondness and longing for the rustic flavor of the dish. Trying it for the first time, Nagoyan picked up a flat dumpling with his chopsticks and said with an air of displeasure, "These aren't dumplings, they're noodles. Botched noodles."

"They're called dumplings."

"I'd call it a primitive sort of miso-simmered udon."

"Is that really so tasty?"

"It's a hundred times more refined than this. First of all, the miso is different. Besides, I can't resist the chewy texture of udon."

I've never eaten Nagoya-style udon noodles, but *refined*? However, in a locality where ingredients were hardly fresh, culinary disguise had, I suppose, been honed to an art. Whenever the geezers in our ward discussed food, they would invariably raise that kind of argument. It occurred to me that Nagoyan must really like the food of his birthplace, but I had little idea about it myself and sensed that if I asked, I would be given a peevish lecture, so I simply sucked up the last of the savory dumplings.

"How 'bowt seein' the *magaibutsu*?

"The *magaibutsu?*"

"Ye know, Buddhas carved into the stone cliff. Enormous they are, as I remember."

From Fukidera we again followed the signs, and before long, there it was. We left the car in the parking lot and took the path up the slope to the entrance, where we found a lot of bamboo canes left in a stand. These were quite helpful, I realized, as we began our climb up the steep rock stairs. Soon we were panting. The tourists on their way back down invariably greeted us. Remembering that such is the custom among mountain hikers, I responded in kind.

A man in a straw hat called out as he passed, "Look out fer th' *igamushi!*"

"Y…yes, we will," I answered without any feeling of concern, not knowing what he was talking about. We went on climbing.

Nagoyan abruptly paused and wheezed, "I've had it! I really don't get what's with you hikers! I love Mt. Fuji, but I'm not about to *climb* it! People go trudging on for hours and hours. And it's pure agony to begin with!"

"We're almos' there," I said and set off again. Nagoyan grumpily followed.

We came to the end of the stone steps and saw an open space immediately before us. A huge *magaibutsu* carved into the façade of the gray cliff was glaring down on us. The facial features were so precise that at first glance one might have thought that it had been formed in a cement mold and then somehow attached to the rock wall. Next to it was another carved figure, a somewhat smaller, delicate Buddha. The first one was a bit intimidating; with his large nostrils, he had a free and easy air about him.

Nagoyan read the signs, exclaiming, "My goodness, these are Acala and Mahavairocana Tathagata. Carved, it says, nine hundred years ago. Awesome!"

In front of the figures was a small vacant lot, the size of a residential park. We sat down on a bench and mopped away the sweat.

"No one's here."

"Rain?"

As I looked up at the cloudy sky, we were hit by a squall of huge drops. The next instant, I couldn't believe my eyes. The drops in which we were being drenched were not of water. Transparent and cold, they seemed to resemble soft jelly beans, though curved like ancient ornamental beads. They stuck to my arms, my calves, and to my T-shirt, and even when they fell to the ground, they did not spread and flow. It appeared that a swarm of slugs had fallen from the sky.

"Heeey!" Nagoyan screamed. "Hana-chan! Blood!"

He was standing motionless. The slugs that thickly covered his cheeks and arms were beginning to take on a dark and murky color. I was frantically trying to tear them off, one at a time, from my face and the nape of my neck. It was hard to do, as they were slimy and rubbery.

When at last I had managed to rid myself of one, blood started dripping down onto my fingers. When after quite a struggle I had flung it down, I saw it curl up on the ground, swollen and reddish-black.

"They're not slugs! They're leeches. Blood-suckin' leeches!"

"Eeeeeek!" screamed Nagoyan and took off down the stone steps like a bat out of hell. I followed frantically after him. The path was wet, and I kept slipping. Blood mixed with sweat was oozing from the places on my face and knees where I'd been bitten.

From far below I heard Nagoyan screech, "Mountain leeches! *Schistosoma japonicum*!"

"Or they might be trombiculid mites," he went on, still shouting.

For someone who had been panting all the way up, he certainly sounded full of energy now. I was fearfully watching my step and unable to keep up.

"They've just changed the name of the scrub typhus pathogen from Rickettsia to Orientia."

"Nagoyan, wait!"

I was slow in making my way to the parking lot. And just as I got there, a speeding white Luce flashed by me, screeching its tires, and tore away down the slope.

"No way!" I wailed. But the gravel-strewn parking lot was empty. I was standing there abandoned in the middle of nowhere.

I looked at my arms and saw no more leeches. Had they been *igamushi*? I rubbed my face with a towel, but there wasn't any more blood. And it wasn't just from my arms that the leeches were gone; I couldn't find a single one anywhere. They'd disappeared as if they'd been a mirage to begin with. But whatever they had been, the fact remained that I was now alone. The sky was overcast, and from out of the thicket came the song of a warbler.

As the shock gradually wore off, I realized that I had no idea what to do in this deserted place. The small shop was closed, perhaps merely for its weekly closing day, though for all I knew it had long since gone out of business.

Nagoyan had run off, ditched me. And here I was in the middle of hilly, uninhabited nowhere. It was really too much. I wondered how many hours it would take me to walk back down to civilization. How would I get off Kunisaki? I hadn't much money. What was I to do?

Twenty yards of linen are worth one coat.

Whenever I was alone, that voice would intrude. It only aggravated my anxiety.

Twenty yards of linen are worth one coat.

With a low rumble, the Luce returned. Nagoyan leaned over the passenger seat and opened the window.

"Forgive me! I just panicked," he said.

At that, I instantly boiled over. "Ye panicked, did ye? Well, ye make me bloody sick! Is that any way fer a man t' act? Screamin' like a halfwit and then runnin' off. Whit did ye expect me to do in this godforsaken place?"

Nagoyan quietly opened the door, got out, and came over to stand in front of me.

"I'm really sorry."

Seeing him tower over me made me all the more incensed. My entire body was seething.

"I didn't know what I was doing. Being attacked b...by a bunch of horrible annelids..."

Nagoyan was genuinely frightened. His features were frozen, and his voice was as brittle as cigarette ash. But I was still as angry as ever.

"And that excuses ye? Ye do whitever ye like 'n then think everythin' will be fine if ye jus' say yer sorry. Yer disgustin', y'are!"

"What else can I do but apologize."

"I don' care fer ye. Don' care none fer ye. Ye might as well die!"
I had been shouting and raging until my mouth was dry.
"I lost my head. I'm sorry. I won't do it again."
"I don' believe ye, and I still don' care fer ye!"
Turning around, I saw a Coca-Cola vending machine. It was filled with the carcasses of small, dead insects. Quite ignoring Nagoyan, I bought a can. He and his car were right behind me, but I was nonetheless overwhelmed by loneliness and self-pity. I wept, raising my head as I sniffled, my tears blending with the carbonated liquid.

Desperate to escape this horrid peninsula, I got into the car and was suddenly seized by a violent headache. It was as if small pebbles were banging against each other within my skull. It was impossible to think. I sat there in the passenger seat, muttering "My head's gonna burst," as I did my best to endure the pain.

"Yikes!" Nagoyan kept saying, jerking the steering wheel back and forth. "This is weird. Aren't we back where we were before?"

With every U-turn, he became more confused. I was holding my head with both hands. The road was meandering through the strangely shaped hills. Feeling utterly miserable, I could hear that voice, now revved up to a terrible tempo.

Twenty yards of linen are worth one coat.
Twenty yards of linen are worth one coat.

It took us over an hour to get to Route 10 – or at least that was how it felt. Once we found ourselves in the stream of traffic, my headache eased.

In Kyushu, Route 10 is indeed of a very different order from Route 3. The artery that arcs around the island to join Kita-Kyushu and Kagoshima is forever fiercely, feverishly throbbing.

"It says that Beppu is this way. Do you want to go there?" Nagoyan asked diffidently.

"Aye. Th' way I'm feelin', I could use a dip in the hot springs."

"They call it hell."

"More like heaven."

It didn't take us long to get there. We stopped at a UNIQLO

outlet, where I bought a brassiere, sweat shorts, a small tote bag, and, for a thousand yen, three pairs of underwear. Not having much money, that was all I could afford.

We then went to Takegawara Hot Springs, housed in a dilapidated wooden building reminiscent of a temple or an old primary school. I ducked under the curtain hanging in front of the women's section and immediately found myself in the dressing room. A set of stairs led down to the dark brown-gray stone baths. The spring was bubbling up into the ancient, U-shaped tub.

I had a towel and one of the fresh T-shirts I had borrowed from Nagoyan, but without either soap or shampoo, I simply poured hot water over myself, feeling somewhat perplexed, until a slender, dark-complexioned woman next to me offered to lend me what she had. When I thanked her, she asked in broken Japanese whether I had come with my boyfriend. It didn't seem to me that there was any need to tell her the truth, so I mumbled "Uh-huh." She smiled back at me.

In the bath I stretched out my arms and legs to the full and felt myself being gently purged of the horrid memory of being eaten alive by the leeches. I wanted to believe that it had all been unreal. The ceiling was high, with latticed windows running all the way to the top, and though we were in a semi-basement, there was just the right hint of sunshine.

I had been too hard on Nagoyan. Whatever had happened, I had somewhat overreacted. No one, including me, has the right to tell another to drop dead. I resolved that once out of the bath I would apologize to him. But as I was thinking about it all, I began to feel dizzy and then things went from bad to worse. All I can remember is crawling back to the dressing room, with everything growing black about me, and, still half wet, putting on the new pair of underwear and the T-shirt that smelled of Nagoyan.

When I came to, I was lying on the tatami mats in the reception hall. When I tried to get up, I heard Nagoyan's voice, "No, no, take it easy." And then after a while the foreign woman brought a cold compress for me. Nagoyan thanked her and then placed it on my forehead.

"I'll be watching the telly. Rest a bit more."

As I lay there with my eyes closed, I could hear the sound of a sumo broadcast.

When eventually I had regained my strength, we made our way back to Route 10. Though we said something about stopping for the night, I had no wish to go to another hot springs, and the alternative – some forlorn business hotel – was likewise unappealing. The road as we left Oita City and headed for Takeda was pitch black; to our left and right, all we could see in the car headlights was thicket. I had the palpable sensation of being in the midst of nature.

Imagining our surroundings, I remarked, "We'll be able to see Mt. Aso tomorrow."

"Oh? Have we come that far already?"

Nagoyan, who seemed to ignore the map as a matter of principle, was simply following the signs, as though he hadn't a clue as to where we were at any given moment.

"Aso is the greatest volcano in the world."

"But Mt. Fuji is Number One in Japan."

"All Fuji's got is height. Aso's bigger than ye can imagine."

"What? Fuji's beautiful, more beautiful than all else in Japan."

Nagoyan was spouting nonsense, as he was sure to learn for himself in the morning.

"Can ye see Mt. Fuji from Nagoya?"

"No, but in the neighborhood of my boarding house in Tokyo, I could see it quite clearly."

"Is that so?"

Nagoyan was an incurable Tokyo nerd. He was so intent on becoming a Tokyoite that he had even embraced local mountain worship. But then, there are those English-literature department types who blabber away in the language, read anything written in it too, and regard themselves as virtual Americans. They're all nuggets too.

7

Nagoyan was already awake when I opened my eyes. We were again parked in a rest area.

"Had a rough night," he remarked. "Couldn't sleep."

To me, the morning seemed rather promising. The night before, though it had been too dark for us to recognize anything, we had at some point made our way into the Aso region. Dark-green clumps were scattered about, but elsewhere was the color of bright, burgeoning grass. Amidst it all was nestled the soft form of the mountains.

"Let's go t' Daikan Peak."

"Where's that?"

"It's there ye have the best view of Aso. Ye don' wanna miss it!"

I had added that in any case it was "on the way," though I hadn't the foggiest as to where we were on our way *to*.

In the parking lot, we nonchalantly wedged the Luce in among the variously colored cars and, mingling with family groups on holiday, briskly headed from the somma rim to the observation platform jutting out like a promontory.

From the tip, one looks down the plain stretching out below or directly across, to the five peaks towering into the sky. Then there is the three hundred and sixty-degree view of the somma. An immense sight, indeed.

"Woooooh! Is this all Aso?"

Nagoyan raised his voice in excitement. Such a reaction to seeing Mt. Aso seemed only natural. It occurred to me that if those peaks had their own voices, they too would resound with "wooooh" and "aaaaah"... The meaning of this escaped me, the mind of the mountains being quite beyond my comprehension.

"There in th' distance... Can ye make it out? The somma goes that far... The entire mountain ring there erupted to form the caldera."

"The somma really goes all around?"

"Indeed it does."

"How big is it?"

"I dunno. Even seein' it, I still can't quite get my head 'round it."

"The inside is flat, I see."

On the enclosed plain were neatly delineated rice and vegetable fields, with towns stretching out here and there, as though someone had drawn fine lines on a blueprint with hard pencil lead. Over the rice fields lay bands of shadows cast by the clouds, and the peaks were wreathed in belching smoke. The eye extended as far as the southern somma, where time too seemed to stop.

All was placid and peaceful.

The tourists all around us likewise wore happy and pleasant expressions. There was no hint of urban discord. Glancing to one side, I saw an otherwise dicey-looking skinhead type holding hands with his brassy babe, a smile on his face.

"My sense of scale seems to have gone quite out of kilter," remarked Nagoyan.

Seeing it all, one couldn't help feeling very small indeed.

"That's whit Mt. Aso does t' ye."

"Where's the crater?"

"Prob'ly over there. That's the central peak."

"Let's go to take a look then," Nagoyan remarked with uncharacteristic resolve.

"It's not a pretty sight, ye know."

"Doesn't matter. I'd like to see it."

I love standing on Daikan Peak and gazing into the distance at Mt. Aso, but the fact is that ever since my childhood, there's been an element of fear about the place. And that's because whenever I went on kiddie club or youth group outings, I would hear stories about the monster cats that haunt their namesake mountain, Nekodake. As a result, I often had nightmares of finding myself about to be killed and devoured by a huge feline beast. Being directly at the crater itself would intensify my anxiety, but now that I was a full-fledged adult, it would hardly do to explain any of this to a first-timer to the area. After all, compared to the horror of mental illness, the crater would be a piece of cake.

As we were coming down from the peak, we spotted a patrol car. Nagoyan gasped.

"We won't be arousin' suspicion, as long as we jus' act normal."

It passed us by without pausing.

The road ended at Daikan Peak. What had they come for, if not to catch us? Just for the trip?

"Whit are we to do at the crater?" I asked, taking advantage of the opportunity to pose the question once more.

"I just want to go there."

"But it's a dead-end road. If the cops come by, we'll be sittin' ducks."

"No problem. That patrol car was just idling by. It had no interest in us."

Nagoyan was obviously of the "danger past, God forgotten" variety.

"Look! Cows!" said Nagoyan cheerily. "Black ones too." And with that he nonchalantly sped off.

"What a splendid prairie this is! Say, how about stopping for a bite to eat?"

We never knew when a cop might show up, but nonetheless he pulled into the Kusasenri rest house.

I was full of trepidation, but then I spotted a sign advertising *ikinari dango*, and now anxiety was quite replaced by a sense of nostalgia. The last time I had been here, I had missed the chance. I felt that now I had seen them I wouldn't let them go for anything. Those precious dumplings were like a beau from whom I had been parted before I could say that I loved him.

I gushed and blabbered on in that vein, but Nagoyan looked totally blank, as could only be expected. The only way to know 'em is to try 'em.

"What *are* they?"

"Instant bean-jam buns, with sliced *batatas* in the filling too. Sweet on th' inside, slightly salty on th' outside. Makes ye feel that ye've never eaten anythin' like it afore. It's one o' the local specialties, like *karashi-renkon*, 'cept that if ye've come to Kumamoto, it's one ye simply can't pass up!"

I was much too eager to eat than to bother with descriptions. I bought five at a hundred yen apiece.

"So what's with the 'instant' part of it?" Nagoyan asked with an air of suspicion.

"Dunno, but I s'pose it means that when batatas suddenly appear, it's a sign that one's about to have a happy encounter with something really delicious… Let's eat 'em on top o' the mountain. They're still too hot now."

"What *is* all this? First it's dumplings in broth, then instant dumplings. And none of them are real dumplings at all!"

"Hereabouts, everythin's called a dumplin'."

"Are they good?"

"Scrumptious! Not whit ye'd call haute cuisine, but something that's near an' dear to the heart."

I was oblivious to all else as we returned to the car. Nagoyan grudgingly followed, muttering, "and what about a meal?" Yet the speed at which he drove to the summit seemed to belie his mood.

As we got out of the car, our nostrils were assailed by the smell of sulfur. The green landscape we had just had before us was gone, and now we were looking at a harsh and austere world of bare rock and gravel, brownish-red and grey.

"It's like the Grand Canyon."

"The Grand Canyon wouldn't 'ave smoke spewin' out."

The people forming a semicircle along the edge of the cone-shaped crater resembled a distant funeral procession, their figures no larger than grains of rice. From their side, thick, white smoke was spouting forth. There was an eerily howling wind but otherwise no sound. It was all quite overwhelming.

"What's that?"

"They're called *tochka*. That's where ye run to when there's an eruption."

There was something indeed quite scary about these round, concrete bunkers. It was terrifying even to contemplate having to take refuge in such a place from molten lava and volcanic smoke. And the word itself, with all its military connotations, somehow suggested a state of emergency. Curious, Nagoyan went off to look at them, only to report that there was nothing there. I replied that they were something like air-raid shelters and nothing more, though, in fact, I had never seen inside one myself.

We trudged over to where we could see the crater. It occurred to me that if we blended into the crowds, we'd be safe from capture. After all, wasn't that what regular crooks did?

The direction of the smoke changed with the shifting of the wind. Far, far below, beneath a slope of scattered boulders and gravel, was the pond-like crater, nestled in level rock. The brimming, moss-green liquid was boiling and bubbling. Could there also be green lava? It lay so far below the point where we stood that all sense of distance was lost, along with any comprehension of the crater's real size.

"I once thought of coming here and throwing myself in," said Nagoyan, his eyes fixed on the sight below.

"*What*? Where did ye get that idea 'n when?"

"Recently."

Flabbergasted, I stared Nagoyan in the face, but he said nothing.

"Waddya mean by 'recently'? Since we've run away?"

My heart was pounding. All this time – from when we first left the parking lot at Takamiya, to when we were driving along the old Route 3, to when I lay awake, unable to sleep, as we camped along the road – Nagoyan was thinking of suicide. And then I had told him to drop dead. I had been so horribly cruel to him!

"But now," he added with a beaming smile, "I see that it's impossible to jump from here. I thought that there would be a moment of pain, but that then it would be over. In fact, it would obviously be quite excruciating. By the time you got to the bottom, you'd have hurt yourself badly and be all bloody."

Human beings want death at a bargain, and I include myself among those who quite detest the thought of going out with any sort of discomfort.

"Ye'd be sure to get yerself stuck along the way 'n then scream fer help."

"I don't 'scream'."

"Oh, but there's not a day that ye don't!"

Nagoyan again gazed pensively down into the crater.

"Unbelievable. I had no idea."

"The world's only."

I had forgotten just *what* it was the world's only, but I was bursting with pride.

We came full circle and found ourselves standing in front of a sign describing the legendary gods of Aso.

"How absurd!" Nagoyan exclaimed. "The usual story has the gods throwing fireballs and creating mountains. But here they come down and act like pioneers, becoming the ancestors of the people who live here now. So who created the heavens and the earth anyway?"

I didn't know what to do with that sort of big question, so I reached into my tote bag, took out the dumplings, and held them out for him.

"So are ye in a better mood now?"

He said nothing, but grabbed one and stuffed it into his mouth.

"Ugh!" he grunted, looking up.

"No way!" I replied. I ate my own, unable to restrain my eagerness for the soft, crumbly taste I so fondly remembered.

"First of all, it's miserably shaped, and then all that's in it is sweet potato."

"But still better than *nagoyan*."

"For someone who's never had that, you're some authority! It's quite the contrary!"

"Ah," I replied laughing, "yer such a fierce defender of your beloved *nagoyan*!"

"All right then," he grumped, "from now on I'll call you 'Ikinari'."

He wolfed down the remaining dumplings and then, looking out over the crater, shouted, "All things considered, it's just ridiculous!"

His laughter made me laugh as well.

"That… *that* is a Porsche! It's a Carrera 4. Isn't it chic?"

We had returned to the parking lot. Nagoyan pointed with his chin to a black vehicle sporting Chikuho plates.

"Whit a frog face it's got!"

"You have no idea."

I plopped myself down in the driver's seat and started the car, quite forgetting that the wheels of the parked Luce were sharply turned and that I needed to put in the clutch. We lurched forward. Nagoyan screamed, and simultaneously there was a startlingly loud crunch. The engine stalled, and there we were, smack up against the black Porsche. In a mindless panic, I turned the key again and put my foot to the accelerator. Again, a tremendous thud. I turned the wheels in the opposite direction, put the car in second gear, and looked to my right. There was a huge dent in the Porsche's door, and the side-view mirror was hanging from a wire. I had somehow managed to do all of that.

"Come on, Hana-chan!" Nagoyan shouted. "Let's get out of here!"

Without even nodding, I hastily drove the car out of the parking lot and headed down the hill. When we came to the fork in the road, I turned in the opposite direction of where we had come from. Lickety-split we were fleeing the scene, the car picking up speed on the slope and veering wildly around each curve in the road. The peril was palpable, like the grip of pitch-black, throbbing mania.

"Hey, it looks like I'd better take charge," said Nagoyan, unable to watch me drive. With his able hands now again at the wheel, we had a smoother path of escape. There were few cars coming towards us from the other lane, and there was no one ahead or behind.

"Remember that gangster-looking type back at the crater? I'm sure that was his car. That is *bad*! If he had caught us, he'd have beaten us to a pulp… And then maybe stuffed us into gasoline drums, set us in concrete, and heaved us into Beppu Bay."

Nagoyan went on grumbling, but I was still petrified. My heart was pounding, my arms and legs were cold, and I was drenched in sweat. In that terrible state, I could hear The Peas cheerfully singing.

Let's stay together
And take that extra mile,
With happiness at last.
Forget the fretting;
Forget the carping.
It's time to lighten up!

"Nagoyan, I'm sorry."

"Huh?"

"I'm no good as a driver, and now I've smushed yer car."

"My Mercedes? No problem. A dent or a scratch on it is a badge of honor. Besides," he added, "it's not that you're 'no good as a driver'; you're something below that: an unlicensed driver."

"An' now I'm aw the more afraid o' getting' caught by the police."

"No need for that."

I had fallen into a kind of funk. In southern Aso, there might not be any car with Chikuho plates coming our way. No, not at all. The hoodlum, his face grim as death, would be scouring Fukuoka and Kumamoto.

I didn't know what lay south of southern Aso. Perhaps there was nothing. South was our only direction.

I was in a state of exhaustion. What little strength I had still had before I faded into oblivion was already dissipating, and I was agonizingly expending it on escape. The alternative was to go back and expiate my sins, bombarded with questions from everyone around and reprimanded by the doctors. But I sensed that to endure hospital life, with its nutcases and all its loathsome realities, was quite beyond my power.

Nagoyan slowed, as we passed over a minor crossing.

"I wonder where the trains along this line go," he asked in a blurry voice.

"To nowhere, pr'aps?"

It seemed unlikely that there would be any train connections south of Aso. In a small, forgotten hamlet were snug clumps of houses, each resting on a low, stone foundation, with red and yellow canna lilies blooming in the corners of the lots, breaking and scattering the light. At the end of a narrow road, we could see a summerhouse.

"I wonder if it's a park."

"Hmmm…"

We parked the car along the roadside nearby. At the base of the summerhouse was a fountain, set in square-forming rock. There were stepping stones, and as we stood in the middle, we could see neatly aligned aquatic plants swaying with the flow of the water. A dipper was hanging from the ceiling.

"This is a spring," said Nagoyan.

"So it must be awright to take a drink."

The cold water, as though penetrating to the recesses of our clavicles, was wonderfully delicious. As we each emptied the dipper, we both smiled.

8

Inside my head a lot of people have suddenly arisen. The ambience is nothing like the calm that reigned on mornings in the hospital ward. I am seized with cold shakes, a loathsome sensation. Some have already been up for some while, and others are following suit. They are always the same persons, but though I recognize their faces and their voices, I do not know their names, and so I call them A, B, and so on.

E is a slight lass, clutching a doll and sobbing, throwing a massive tantrum. F, an older female about 30, is trying to soothe her. The scariest for me is B, a short, muscular male.

"That's one we just have to kill," he says.

"But if you do that, what'll become of us?" asks C, a middle-aged weakling in a suit.

I'm the one to whom B is referring. They're having a discussion about killing me.

"If we drive her to suicide," B replies, "we'll be in the clear. Can't have it be an accident or anything like that."

H, acting as the secretary, peers through his glasses as he takes notes of the meeting.

"Doesn't deserve to live! Hurry up with it!" F is screaming hysterically.

E has stopped crying. A is sound asleep. D says nothing.

"Anyway, we just need to keep pushing," says B. "We've been doing well so far. We can't afford to make a mess of it as we did last time."

Now G pipes up, "The more she runs, the closer we get to 'er." I never actually see him; I can only hear his voice.

I want it to stop. I want it to disappear. I'm being hijacked. It's all inside of me, but I'm not there. I look for my own voice, but it's no good. I can't find it.

I have the premonition that when this powerful delusion eases, I'll still find it terribly irksome to go on living. And that's just what those blokes are aiming for.

Twenty yards of linen are worth one coat.

Twenty yards of linen are worth one coat.

The only thing I have realized is that the voice is the same as G's.

Twenty yards of linen are worth one coat.

Twenty yards of linen are worth one coat.

Already from some time before, G had, in fact, clearly emerged into the surface of my consciousness, like a worm breaking out of an apple.

A long day, an endless afternoon…

The car was heading along a broad bypass toward Takamori.

"It's no good. I'm feelin' creepy."

"Symptoms of mania?"

"Uh-huh… Hard t'explain."

"Were you able to sleep last night?"

"Fer about three hours. I woke up right away."

"If you're sleepy, take a nap. You can lean the seat back."

Twenty yards of linen are worth one coat.

"Uh. When I get worked up, I can't sleep. An' once I'm in a rage ower nothin', I wish I still had a cell phone, as there're a lot o' people I'd call up 'n let fly at, even some I've not seen fer a long time. An' I'd tell 'em, I want no more t' do wit' ye!"

"Yes, but once over your mania, you'd regret it. Just as well you don't have that cell phone."

Twenty yards of linen are worth one coat.

Twenty yards of linen are worth one coat.

"'Get it out!' it says."

"Says who?"

"My brain matter. So that it can't get into my head."

"Yeah. I don't understand it, but I can see that it's really bad. I would have thought mania would be fun, but I was dead wrong."

"Mania too is grim awright."

"Yeah."

"It's so intense. Whit t' do? I feel all at sea!"

"Well, for the time being, since we're on the run, we'll be all right where we are."

"Where are we?"

"In the car. For now, this is home."

His words were kind, but they didn't get through to me.

Twenty yards of linen are worth one coat.

"Oh! Would ye mind if I screamed?"

"I'll grant you a triple indulgence."

Nagoyan elegantly smiled, again only with his mouth.

"It's like bein' in a railway carriage that's gone careenin' outa control. There's nothin' ye can do t' brake, so I'm afraid it's bound t' go down the slope 'n derail."

"Like in the Mitaka Incident."

"Whit's that?"

"It was during the Occupation. An unmanned train derailed in the small hours. It's all a mystery, like the Shimoyama and Matsukawa incidents, which occurred about the same time. There are a lot of theories, but none of it's ever been proved..."

The wings of Nagoyan's nose, I could see, were twitching. But I could not get into such ancient lore, being primarily concerned with my own immediate problems.

"Am I a friggin' pain in th' arse?"

Nagoyan did not reply. I suppose no matter what he'd said, I would have become all the more confrontational – truly a pain, not just irritating. Perhaps he was being silent because he didn't know what I was talking about. Or perhaps he thought that I'd pretty well described myself. There was no end to the turmoil inside my head, and trying to put the best face on it wouldn't do any good. I simply had to take my medicine and wait for the storm to pass. My doctor had warned me that medication would not alone cure me, but I had no strength left to go on fighting on my own, without cover. Yet I had no Limas available. And even if I had had some, it would, unlike stomach medicine, take a while to kick in. I was losing all sense of proportion and felt like a rubber band stretched to its limit. A single sarcastic remark might have been enough to send me into a rage.

Twenty yards of linen are worth one coat.

Twenty yards of linen are worth one coat.

"I'm worried about me meds."

"We only have three doses of Rohypnol left."

"I want some Mellaril too."

"Here in the middle of the mountains, there's nothing we can do about that."

Nagoyan stopped the car at a large drugstore along the bypass. Not feeling in the mood to go into a pharmacy that didn't sell what I wanted, I lowered the car seat and rested, wrestling with the refrain of "Twenty yards of linen"…in my head.

Nagoyan did not return for quite a long time, but when he did, he happily showed off his purchases.

"Look! I've bought a picnic cooler. Ice, scissors, rope, a utility knife, mayonnaise, shampoo, body soap… And here – fireworks."

Except for the shampoo and soap, these items were all forbidden in the hospital.

I was suspicious.

"What're ye goin' t' do wit' all that?"

"It'll come in useful when we steal vegetables… Besides, I really want to do some laundry."

"Whit do ye want wit' fireworks?"

"We can have some fun with them at night. In any case, we're both bored."

I hadn't eaten any of the dumplings at Kusasenri, so by now I was feeling hungry. We lost no time in seeking out a field where no one was in sight. There we nobbled some tomatoes and cucumbers, washing them down with the spring water we had kept in plastic bottles. Our stomachs were gurgling. What we had left over we put into the cooler.

At the town office in Takamori, I used the restroom. As we came out again from the parking lot, we spotted a strange sign and exchanged glances: *Nekoyama Mental Clinic*. A strange name, evoking feline-haunted hills. Pondering whether it was for real, we followed the sign ever further along a cedar-lined road, until we eventually found ourselves standing in front of a white, Western-style building that looked as though it had been plucked from the late nineteenth century and neatly plunked down in the middle of this cedar forest. Inside the dome-topped wooden door there was only a red velvet sofa set against the white wall of the hall, across from which was a frosted glass panel. A young woman opened it with a grating sound and greeted us. As the window was small, all we could see was her fox-like eyes. I wondered whether she too was a member of the cat clan.

She asked for a health insurance certificate, and when Nagoyan said in loud voice that we'd forgotten it, she gave him an indifferent look and then had him write down our names and address. He falsely stated us to be Daisuke and Kiyomi Shimada. Sure enough, the first name that popped out of his head was *hers*. I wished he had used a bit of imagination and come up with something more elegant. For an address, he put down Akasaka in the Chuo Ward of Fukuoka, no doubt with the location of his company in mind.

Other than ourselves, there was no one in the waiting room. After a while, we were summoned by a deep, low voice into the examination room. We went in and were met by a large figure dressed in white. His tousled hair gave him the appearance of Beethoven. I had thought I would laugh if it turned out that he had a feline appearance to match his name; in fact, he resembled rather the largest member of the species.

Nagoyan offered salutations, and then we sat down in adjacent chairs that appeared quite small in comparison with the one in which the doctor was seated.

Dr Lion gave us both, first me, then Nagoyan, a sharp glance, his bushy eyebrows twice moving up and down.

"Deserters, eh?" he thundered. I had the feeling that were he to talk atop a mountain, his voice would be so loud that one would hear the echo forever.

"No, no, we've just moved and haven't taken care of our papers... This is my younger sister..."

The more Nagoyan spoke, the fishier his story sounded. Anyone would have been able to see through it all.

"I once thought about deserting, myself... It was during that war awhile back."

He laughed heartily, so that we could not help giggling ourselves.

"Did you succeed...?" Nagoyan asked him.

"I wouldn't be alive today if I *had* succeeded. I went to where I'd been sent to deliver a dispatch and then tried to take off, but after agonizing about it, I wound up returning. Trouble was that I got back to the barracks after curfew, and that cost me a beating and two hard nights in the brig.

"Oh…"

"Well, that was the army for you. Of course, if I'd actually gone through with my plan to desert and then been caught, I suppose they would've put me up in front of a firing squad. Fortunately, I didn't get sent off to battle. The transport ship didn't arrive. Probably torpedoed and sunk in the South Seas. And while we were waiting, the war ended. And even after that, times were tough…"

We still hadn't got down to business.

As the doctor was telling us the story of his life, I wondered whether *we*'d be able to go on living. *Twenty yards of linen are worth one coat. Twenty yards of linen are worth one coat. Twenty yards of linen are worth one coat.* Sweat had broken out and was running down my neck and into my T-shirt. Suddenly, I found myself talking.

"Doctor, I suffer from an auditory hallucination when I'm manic. And then it gets worse. I don't know what I'm doing. *Twenty yards of linen are worth one coat.* I hear it each and every day, and I don't understand what the meaning of it all is."

"What is it you hear?"

"Twenty yards of linen are worth one coat."

"Oh," he replied, running his hand through his sparrow's-nest hair. "That's a line from *Shihonron*. It used to be rendered a bit differently. Of course, I didn't read it myself until long after… In the postwar era. And now that I think about it, I suppose the translation has changed…"

He reminisced, oblivious of his audience.

"Doctor, I'm really disturbed by it. I'm even more terrified by the hallucinations. I can't express just *how* terrified… Doctor, please give me some Mellaril."

"What are the symptoms of those hallucinations?"

"There are all kinds. I have a lot of people jabbering away in my head. It's scary. It seems that if I say anything, I'll get even more. That makes it all the worse."

"Does Mellaril stop the hallucinations?"

"The visual ones, yes; the auditory ones, no."

For mania, Dr Lion told me, he would prescribe Limas, to be taken after breakfast, lunch and dinner, and then again before bedtime. I was very relieved that he made no mention of Tetropin; I sensed that he knew it to be a bad drug.

"What sleeping remedy works for you?"

"Rohypnol and Levotomin. But I suffer from early morning awakening."

"Have you ever taken Vegetamin?"

"I used to take Vegetamin A, and it really worked, but they wound up refusing to give it to me."

Dr Lion made a mischievous face.

"You took it all at once, didn't you?"

I inadvertently nodded. Nagoyan nudged me with his elbow to warn me that that was a bad move.

Turning to him, the doctor said, "Can you promise me not to take your eyes off your sister until you've both returned to Fukuoka?"

Nagoyan timidly bobbed his head in agreement.

"You two have let off enough steam. Now be good and go back."

"Yes, Doctor," I said.

After a moment's silence, Nagoyan asked, "You won't notify them or anything, will you?"

The doctor again burst out with the laughter of an imp in tales of long ago.

"Why would I do that?"

Nagoyan explained that he was largely on the mend and that all he needed was a few measly medicines, including some barbiturates.

The doctor carefully posed some questions concerning the onset and progress of his illness and the drugs that he had had been prescribed.

"How about sleep?"

"It's better than before, but when I wake up at daybreak, I feel terribly anxious."

"I see."

"Actually, until recently I thought it would be better for me to kill myself..."

To this Dr Lion roared back, "No, you're not to take the big baby's way out!"

We jumped in surprise, but with this anger passed, and he immediately resumed in his normal voice.

"You have to be aware that it takes a remarkably long time to recover from depression. You have to take everything slowly, without making any hasty decisions."

Having said this, he fell silent for a while and then, in a sober tone, bade us farewell.

We assumed that there would be a pharmacy nearby, but the fox-eyed assistant handed us our medicine along with the bill. The ingredients were the same; only the manufacturer was different. They were all generic products. The consultation fee, which Nagoyan paid, was alarmingly high.

When we got back to the car, I immediately took some Mellaril and some Limas. Counting up the capsules, we realized we had only been given a week's worth. "How stingy!" I thought, whereupon Nagoyan remarked with a nonchalant expression on his face, "Well, well, you're perfectly capable of speaking properly after all, with all the polite inflections to boot."

"'Course I can."

"What now? Are we going to do as the doctor told us to?"

"No, I can't do that."

I hadn't the slightest inclination to go back. The Nekoyama Clinic had been really just a medical supply depot. We were directionless, string-cut kites.

In a plain and simple restaurant in front of the station in Takamori, we ordered cold noodles. Nagoyan took some of his own mayonnaise from the car and squeezed it over his portion in a zigzagging spiral, as though he were about to eat a Japanese *tarte flambée*.

"Don't you want some too?"

"I don' believe it. Ye put mayonnaise on cold noodles? Disgustin'!"

"Huh? Isn't that the usual way?"

"Is that whit ye aw do in Nagoya?"

Nagoyan grumbled in reply that he did not think it a peculiarly local custom, but he had never thought about the matter before. He didn't seem very confident as he began to slurp his noodles. Then suddenly, with a look of triumph on his face, he exclaimed, "What *are* you talking about? After all, people in Kyushu put Worcestershire sauce on noodles…"

"Right. An' sauce 'n vinegar fer crispy fried noodles is quite normal too."

"Now *that* is genuinely weird! What is absolutely normal is putting mayonnaise on cold noodles."

I couldn't eat my own noodles, even without mayonnaise. The idea of putting anything in my mouth somehow made me queasy. I took two bites and put my chopsticks down. To see Nagoyan so eagerly sucking it all in was revolting.

"Aren't you going to eat?"

I looked sullenly at my uncut nails and wanted to get a manicure. It occurred to me that I might give them a vivid color.

I was going out of control. I was hyper but at the same time feeling utterly miserable. I wanted to throw everything on the floor – my remaining food, the bottle of condiments, the chair that was next to me. And the next object I'd destroy would be me. *Twenty yards of linen are worth one coat. Twenty yards of linen are worth one coat. Twenty yards of linen are worth one coat.*

Nagoyan knew that I was agitated.

"Go for a walk or something," he said and then ordered a coffee. (Cold noodles followed by coffee!…)

"Give me th' key. I'm goin' back to the car."

"All right," thrusting out his right hip in order to put his hand in his pocket.

"But don't start the engine. I don't want to be left stranded here."

"Don' ye trust me?"

Nagoyan made a bluntly unpleasant face and got up. No one was at the cash register. The personnel were perhaps all in the back; in any case, they showed no sign of appearing.

"Let's make a run for it."

Twenty yards of linen are worth one coat. I didn't need a reason to run.

Breaking out in a cold sweat, we stealthily left the restaurant and got into the car. The Luce put one more item on its rap sheet as it roared off in a mad burst of speed. We had done it again.

"And now we've bilked on a bill," he lamented in a tear-filled voice. "How many years will we do if they catch us? And I left my mayonnaise behind…"

"Can't be helped. Ye'll jus' have to buy some more."

"We can't go back now, can we?" he remarked, an expression of resignation on his face.

"How far will we go now?" I asked as I spotted a blue road sign. The question made no sense, but I simply wanted to pose it.

"You're asking me? This was all your idea."

Nagoyan was squinting in obvious annoyance, so I merely muttered that he should just keep going. I had become accustomed to this car. All that I had etched in my brain was the instinct, like that of an arctic tern, to fly on south. Nothing else appeared to make any sense.

9

I made a bit of progress in my driving skills. I got so I could shift into fourth gear. Nagoyan was still at the wheel for any mountain passes we negotiated, but I realized that cars are like computers or cell phones: they're designed for human use. I wanted to take real lessons and get a license. Having passed through a tunnel, we saw no more sign of town life; Takamori may have been the last of it. Yet even if that were true, we were still on the right track. Following the gently looping road, we found ourselves now completely beyond the somma. Before us stretched a range of mountains quite unknown to me. They were not particularly high, but as we crossed one after another, the billowing waves of green seemed to go on forever. Was this what it meant to run away, to escape – to be ever heading to places we did not know, that no one knew?

"I never thought about what's beyond Aso."

"Could it be Mount Kirishima?"

"No way it could be so close by."

There was nothing other than the forest and the road. And no sign of human habitation.

"So what's wi' that *Shihonron?*"

I'd never heard of it before, but an image floated up in my mind of a huge, beautiful Chinese bird cooing *shi-hon-ron.*

"I don't know it. Whit is it?"

"Were you in the faculty of economics?"

"No, in literature, in the English department."

"So I don't suppose you read it."

"Whit is it?"

"It's a Communist text – *Das Kapital* by Karl Marx. I haven't read all of it, but I did take M.E."

"M.E.?"

"Marxist economics. But why do you…? It's all quite mysterious…"

"My ex did economics."

The words were no sooner out of my mouth than Nagoyan shouted, "Then there's no mystery to it at all. How boring! *He* must have read it, and so he's the source. Once you understand that, your hallucination will disappear."

"Rather than reasons, I could use some Mellaril."

I knew this from experience. I'd been told by my doctor as well: "Mental illness strikes both with and without a cause. You fall into the latter category, so instead of digging up the past, you should be thinking about how you're to live from now on."

But had I, in fact, read *Shihonron*? I had no memory of that creepy sentence. Was Tsuyoshi the sort of person who would have encouraged me to read what must be a difficult work? I was trying to forget him but still had the nagging memory of his gratuitous reference to my "mental illness."

"Bein' mental, was I wrong to haf a boyfriend?"

"Why?"

"'Cos as soon as he 'eard of it, he dumped me."

"So that's what happened…"

"E'en though I was behavin' normally."

"Normal people don't understand."

"Then only the sick can hang out wit' the sick…"

"Now you're taking the argument to an extreme. After all, healthy people don't necessarily understand each other either. Hegel says as much."

"Whit does he say?" I asked, observing the wings of Nagoyan's nose.

"Human desires do not exist except in relation to the 'Other,' and as our will or our ideas do not exist purely on their own, it is a mistake to suppose that there can be understanding between oneself and that Other."

"I've no idea whit you're sayin'."

"Well then, never mind about Hegel. The point is that we see only what we want to see."

"Once I'd made my attempt, I wound up losin' nearly aw me friends."

"It doesn't matter. Anyone who ends a friendship over mental illness is someone you're bound to lose sooner or later."

He had spoken generally of friends, but I knew quite well that he meant Tsuyoshi. Still, I didn't know whether I'd ever be able to find another boyfriend if the story about my manic-depression wound up getting broadcast to the world.

"Nagoyan, ye had a girlfriend, didn't ye?"

"Yes, when I was a student. We tried to keep up a long-distance relationship, but it didn't work out. We'd already broken up by the time my illness became apparent, so I don't think she ever knew about it."

"So ye wanna go back to Tokyo?"

"No. I just like Tokyo."

"Whit makes ye like it so much?"

"Hmmm... There are so many places to shop... I suppose it's the volume of information available too. It's got movies, books, everything..."

I tried to follow Nagoyan in the metropolitan scene of my imagination but lost him, and then again heard the voice: *Twenty yards of linen are worth one coat.* How long would it echo in my mind? How long would I have to put up with this illness? Perhaps my case was so dire that what I needed was a powerful drug to turn me into a zombie.

"Ye know, Nagoyan, it's a sad thing, bein' off yer rocker."

"Lavender!" said Nagoyan suddenly. "They say it's good. The smell supposedly calms you down."

"Really?"

"Let's go look for some, the two of us."

It was the first time I heard him refer to "the two of us." Floating up in my mind was the image of us wandering through the faintly purplish haze of a distant highland picking flowers. I felt a pang in my heart and stole a glance at Nagoyan's profile.

How handsome he looked, how gentle and kind. I wondered whether we would find any lavender.

10

It was just noon when the air conditioner went on the fritz. Inside the car we were engulfed in heat – sizzling heat. Nagoyan got out and opened the hood; he stood there with his arms folded, a puzzled expression on his face, then closed it again.

"The long and short of it," he said, announcing the self-evident, "is that the air conditioner has broken down."

"Why of aw times does it break down now? This wreck of a car!"

"Don't belittle my automobile!"

"Aw I meant to say was whit it is!"

"Look. It's hot enough without your getting angry."

"But the reason I'm boilin' over is 'cause it's so bloody hot!"

"All right. Then simmer quietly, because you know you mustn't get yourself really worked up."

"I don' like it…"

We pulled into a service station. When we asked the attendant about the cooler, he pleaded ignorance on behalf of both himself and his colleagues but added, "If ye're members of the Japan Automobile Federation, ye can call…"

Doing that would have betrayed our position. We had the tank filled and then took off.

"As long as it's not a problem with the compressor…"

"Whit's a compressor?"

"It's an automobile part," Nagoyan replied, as though taking me for a fool.

"So we're to go on makin' our escape in the heat?"

"Can't be helped. Let's take the expressway. It should be all right now. We won't be caught."

Nagoyan appeared to be bored with the monotony of the road we were now driving.

"The expressway's on t'other side o' the mountains."

Nagoyan sighed, a look of weary disgust on his face.

"Do you suppose there's a Mazda dealer?"

"D'ye think we'll find one in a place like this?"

"No, I suppose not."

Route 265 steadily narrowed, and then the centerline disappeared. When a car came from the opposite direction, Nagoyan would skillfully back up to a wider area of the road and then move forward again to let ongoing cars squeeze past. He explained that it was a technique known as "coupling and parting."

It was evening when we pulled into Shiiba. A small village, it had a liquor shop but no convenience store, and though it also had a set-menu restaurant, we couldn't very well expect to find a Mazda dealer there. I told Nagoyan that I was sick of sleeping in the car. He agreed, and so we wound up as walk-in guests at a local inn. Again we registered under fake names, this time as Kazuo and Michiko Sato. They had a distinctly unsophisticated sound to them, as if we were already oldsters. Nagoyan had a tin ear.

I felt the accumulated fatigue, my body aching from having been cooped up in the car for so long. Not being in the mood to do anything, we sprawled out in a stupor on the floor of the Japanese-style room until the proprietress came in with our dinner.

"If ye should be needin' more rice, ma'am, just call."

I'd never been spoken to as though I were a married woman before. The beer went straight to my head. I didn't think I had much of an appetite, but as I started to eat the broiled trout and the gourd stew, I relished it all. Nagoyan steadily drank his beer, nibbling on his food. Once he reached out for the television remote control, but then gave up on the idea. There was a small bath attached to the room, but I went instead to the inn's main shared bath facility. Sitting in the hip tub of the tiled bathing room were two shriveled grandmothers with sagging breasts, talking in Miyazaki dialect about love in old age. I kept to myself, concentrating on a thorough scrubbing. Returning to the room, I found the futon already laid out and Nagoyan taking his sleeping medicine. I took mine as well, and then Nagoyan silently turned off all but a small light, as we each, from opposite sides, crawled into our summer bedding. I was heartily sick of pitch-black nights. I could distinctly make out the four corners of the ceiling in the weak yellow light of the electric bulb. Oh, I thought, rooms are nice! Futons are nice. I'd had it with sleeping in the car. I knew what I needed: freedom, a futon, and a little money.

From outside came the clear sound of the insects chirring.

"We're like brother an' sister."

"Brother and sister speaking different languages."

"But we can still do it."

"Nah, thot'd be wrong!"

"Why?"

"If we're not lovers, it's wrong. And it's not just with me you shouldn't be doing it."

"Uh-huh."

I had merely felt sorry for him, thinking that as we had already been together so many nights, I could at least do it for him once. But Nagoyan, like a genuine elder brother, gently said "good night."

I pulled the covers up over my nose to enjoy their well-starched feel. For a moment I suppressed a laugh but then decided that as I'd already downed the pills, I had to say what was on my mind or lose it forever. I pulled back the covers.

"Say…"

"What's the matter? Isn't the medicine working?"

In the semi-darkness, he sounded sleepy.

"Nagoyan, a minute ago you talked different."

Nagoyan yelped and bolted upright. I guffawed, almost losing whatever sleepiness I had gained from the medicine.

"What? No way!"

"But you did." I imitated him.

"Oh, bother!"

I greatly regretted that in the dim light I could not clearly make out Nagoyan's agonized face. Again I suppressed a giggle and then laughed anyway, the cycle repeating itself until at last I fell asleep.

It was a deep sleep with no early morning awakening.

"Aaaah!"

I woke up to Nagoyan calling out. It was already light.

"Aah, aah," he groaned. I glanced over and saw him gingerly raising up his bottom from the futon. When our eyes met, he said, "It's all right. Go back to sleep."

I had a fairly clear idea of what had happened, so I did as I was told, turning my back to him. Nagoyan hastily lifted the futon. I could hear him pushing it into the closet, then pattering off to the bath, and closing the door behind him. As the sound of the water in the shower continued, I speedily changed.

Nagoyan emerged, dressed in his usual change of clothes, a look of nonchalance on his face. He stood by the window and leisurely shaved.

"Did ye pish then?"

"What are you talking about?"

"Ye wet yer bed."

I saw him blush to his ears.

"Now don't get yerself so upset. It's jus' that yer medicine worked too well."

"Well, lass, do ye ever pish yerself?"

He spoke in a low voice, trying unsuccessfully to imitate me. "Lass," he called me, apparently thinking that as he had wet his bed in my presence, it would pretentious to speak more formally.

"Twice or thrice."

"I can't bear it – a grown man like me doing… It's never happened before."

"Shows ye're getting better. Any normal person would be sure to experience the same."

I gave bed-wetter Nagoyan a sidelong glance as I put toothpaste to toothbrush.

"Good thing ye didn't skyte."

"What's that?"

"It's whit ye do when ye're not pishin'."

"Amazing! That one's even better than whatever it is you say for 'goodbye'."

The two words seemed quite unrelated, but it was too much trouble to explain. I returned to the bathroom and briskly brushed my teeth.

11

The road had widened at Shiiba, but thereafter narrowed. Nagoyan was constantly honking the horn, and when I asked why, he said there were "Sound Horn" signs before every curve. I realized that until that moment, I hadn't given any thought to the signs or their meaning. Observing them now as we drove, I saw that each had rusted to dark reddish brown. There was barely room for two-way traffic, and the battered pavement was split down the middle, with a straight line of slender grass growing in the crack.

"That's the median strip," Nagoyan remarked, and when I expressed credulous surprise, he admitted he was joking. Flowing down onto one side of the road was the dark forest, with a natural mixture of soil; on the other side was a cliff of protruding boulders. Stones the size of melons scattered about spoke to the truth of a sign warning of rockslides. As it would have been quite an impossible task for me, Nagoyan was doing all the driving. We stopped the car at a scenic spot and looked out at the endless chain of mountains; in the distance, appearing as small as the edge of a fingernail, the village of Shiiba reflected the light. There was no other sign of human endeavor.

"How far does this road go?" We had been on it for hours since Nagoyan first posed the question.

"Do ye s'pose it might be a forestry road?"

Nagoyan snapped back with an air of authority, "It's National Route 265, and it's the pits! It ought to be called 'abomi-national'!"

"It's a good thing there are no oncoming cars," he continued. "Where in the world would we have to back up to in order to let them by? All we need is to meet a truck, and we'll be finished. What can we do?"

Yet for all his complaining there was no improvement, and the local place name indicated below the road signs we passed remained unchanged: Omata. There's no one living here, I thought. We continued our meandering way, climbing the slopes and descending again into ravines.

With all the twists and turns, I became carsick.

"Stop – anywhere'll do!" I exclaimed.

"Wait until the road widens a bit," Nagoyan replied. He pulled over to the left alongside a stream, where there was a straight stretch. I leaned the seat partway back and remained motionless, waiting to recover. There was not the slightest breeze. I thought that if there was a reoccurrence of my auditory hallucination at that moment, that would really be the end. Nagoyan put on his backpack and headed down into the streambed.

When at last I felt better, I went to join him. He had stepped into clear, blue water and was standing unsteadily, washing the underwear into which he had pissed, along with various other items. He had carefully tied his rope to trees along the bank to serve as a clothesline. Having spread body shampoo on his T-shirt, he was diligently scrubbing, then rinsing.

I laughed as I saw him take a step forward, slip, and fall into the stream, but now as he tried to stand up again, he slipped again. Letting out a scream, he fell into the deeper water.

"Hana-cha—!"

With his head bobbing up and down in the current, he called out, "I...can't...swim!"

Up he spluttered again, struggling to get a hand out of the water, and in that frantic effort sank once more and disappeared.

Nagoyan had been swept away in the current.

I raced back to the car, got in, and started the engine. I had to rescue him. Nagoyan was going to drown! Thinking only of heading him off, I pushed the accelerator to the floorboard and tore off faster than I had ever driven before.

The stream followed the road, descending into a deep gorge. There didn't seem to be anywhere that would allow me to climb down to rescue him... He couldn't bloody swim! How could that be? Unbelievable! He had no business coming to Kyushu if he couldn't! It was summer, and with Itoshima and Hirado just waiting for him, he hadn't bothered to learn...! How stupid could he get?

Now driving alone for the first time ever, I felt every hair standing on end from the tension, even as I felt a mixture of anger and concern. I could not have been underway for more than a few minutes, but the distance I had gone seemed immense. As I went, I could see through the shadow of the trees that the stream had widened. There was a shoal, blending sand and small pebbles, and there the current appeared to slow. Spotting a fisherman's path leading down to the stream, I slammed on the brakes, causing the engine to stall, and yanked up the side brake. If I were to let him slip by, that it would be it. There was no time to lose.

I ran down over the gravel to a simple bridge, consisting of nothing more than planks some five centimeters thick, held together by wire. I wobbled across partway, then jumped down onto what appeared to be a soft, sandy spot. I waded in and stood with my arms spread, the water nearly reaching my underwear, until Nagoyan, having given in to the stream, his eyes rolled back, came floating down. Having taken one of his hands, I put another of my own hands on his shoulder and pulled as hard as I could. "Ouch!" he screamed and tried to stand up on his own, only to slip on the mossy stones of the river bottom.

Wet as rats, we stumbled over the pebbles, trying to catch our breath. But when my heart palpitations had eased, I realized that we had no idea what to do now. My jeans clung heavily, and the parts that the sun was warming gave me an unpleasant feeling.

"Ahhh, I swallowed water!"

"Ye bloody fool!"

"The river took my T-shirt!"

"The hell wit' yer T-shirt!"

"Well, we're not in the ocean, so I knew that eventually I'd be all right."

Saying that, Nagoyan suddenly coughed and, turning downstream, went off to vomit. It seemed he couldn't directly thank me for having saved him. I felt mildly disgusted. If he had said one word of the sort, I might have been able to tell him how glad I was that he hadn't drowned and to feel some sense of relief. Of course, if he had indeed wound up dead, I wouldn't have known what to do.

In the car, I changed out of my wet clothes, and then we went off again to do our laundry. The current wasn't swift, but this time

I didn't let my eye off Nagoyan. I still felt embarrassed to have my panties and bras on display, but it couldn't be helped. For his part, Nagoyan made no bones about hanging up the pants he'd pissed in on a line he again hung between the trees. Only our shoes refused to dry.

We were unusually quiet, waiting until our clothes were half dry. Casually tossing them into the broiling-hot back of the car, we set off again along the wretched road.

We had been driving for quite a while, when we saw the center line reappear for the first time in many an hour. We both let out a shout. Nagoyan immediately put the engine into fourth gear. Connected to the foot of the bridge leading to Tashirobae Dam was a small parking area. It had neither a restroom nor vending machines. There was a pavilion, where a written explanation of the dam was provided. The reservoir was half empty, with a yellowish soil laid bare; it was a truly atrocious sight. Being from subtropical Kyushu, I may be particularly squeamish about any hint of drought.

A blue sign told us that there was a branching prefectural highway that would take us from Aya along the dam to Miyazaki.

"Have you been there?"

"No, never."

"Let's go there to get the air conditioner repaired."

Yet, when following the dam, we turned left at the fork into a narrow road, we encountered an absurdly large electric bulletin board, telling us in thick red letters: **CLOSED TO ALL TRAFFIC DUE TO DISASTER REPAIRS. TO REOPEN DECEMBER**.

"Well, it can't be helped," said Nagoyan, having consulted the map. "There's supposed to be quite a similar road, Prefectural Route 62." Steering back and forth several times, he made a U-turn and took us back to the national highway.

"Even if we have no luck with Route 62," he remarked laughingly, "we can drive straight to Kobayashi." He exuded great confidence, sure of smooth sailing, but we hadn't gone fifteen minutes before we encountered another sign, this one concerning Route 265: **CLOSED TO ALL TRAFFIC DUE TO ROAD SHOULDER COLLAPSE**.

"What is this supposed to mean??" Nagoya exclaimed. For a long time he was silent.

"I'd guess it's been rainin' a lot."

I couldn't understand how, with the low level in the reservoir, the road could be closed. Had all the water leaked out?

"We can't use Route 62 either. What's all this about 'national roads'?"

"Gettin' all steamed up won't do ye any good."

"Am I steamed up? Now I don't think there's much good about Nagoya, but at least it's got a really fine infrastructure. They got started on road planning right after the war. There's a hundred-meter-wide avenue. And even that is overshadowed by the four- and five-lane highways around the Sakae district and Nagoya Station. At least all of that is first-rate."

All this blather wasn't of any use. For the first time in quite a while I was aware of my empty stomach, of acute, penetrating, pressing hunger pangs. There were only two choices before us: to take the road to Taragi in Kumamoto Prefecture or to go back over the same bad road on which we had just come.

"How 'bout goin' through Ebino t' Kagoshima?"

"After all of this," snapped Nagoyan, grinding his teeth, "we're going to Miyazaki no matter what."

"There're hot springs in Kirishima, ye know."

"The first thing is the air conditioning," persisted Nagoyan. "And as we've already decided on Miyazaki, that's where we're going."

"Ye think ye can go do that now?"

Dusk had already fallen, and the day was quite gone. Even the evening cicadas had stopped chirping.

"Can't be done, I suppose," replied Nagoyan in a discouraged tone, turning on the overhead light and looking at the map.

"No, we can't do anymore today," I agreed. "Ye're no doubt tired from th' mountain roads." I added that it would be good if I were able to handle the passes.

"What are you saying?" came the scornful retort. "You haven't even got a license."

The only reasonable thing to do was to go back to the parking lot, with its pavilion, near the Tashirobae Dam. That meant sleeping in the car again. When my eyes had become accustomed to the darkness, I got out without a word and went quickly into the tall grass. Checking behind me, I lowered my jeans and underwear and peed, the hard weeds jabbing at my buttocks.

"I'm hungry," exclaimed Nagoyan.

In the unlit pavilion we sat across from each other, our flashlight between us. There was nothing in our picnic cooler but water. Along the way we had traveled there had been not a single field where we might have stolen some vegetables.

"I'd love to have some meat. We've had nothing but vegetables and fish. We're not old codgers."

"I'd settle fer anythin'."

"I suppose you'd like to be eating your instant dumplings about now…"

"I'd murder some Hyuga chicken."

"Ah, yes! When it comes to meat, I like chicken best."

"Kentucky Fried's awright too, but I don't suppose we'll find any 'round here."

"There's nothing like 'The Restaurant of Many Orders' around here. Say, how many cars passed us today, do you suppose? Maybe not one, the whole day."

Completely missing in Nagoyan's account of "the whole day" was the half day he'd squandered by falling into the stream.

"How I'd jus' love some salted mackerel. That 'n hot rice, salted cod's roe, and miso soup."

"Stop it. I'm hungry. No more talk about food. We still have water."

As for that water, it could go bad in the heat at any time. And I had no desire to drink what was in the muddy reservoir.

"We've got only water and medicine. I feel like a hydrophyte."

At least here in the middle of nowhere we should have been able to feast our eyes on a clear, starry firmament, but unluckily enough, the sky was clouded faintly white. The sweet sound of the croaking frogs was one I had never heard before.

"Pitch black, well, innit now!" I remarked. At this Nagoyan bolted up as though he had just awakened.

"Let's set off some sparklers!"

I remembered that in Takamori, Nagoyan had, on the spur of the moment, bought a package of fireworks and put them in the trunk. Even the small ones, the kind that in the city only small children enjoy, were enchantingly beautiful, emitting dazzling sparks. As the cigarette lighter became too hot to handle, we would use the embers of one device to ignite the next. In the end, there were so many left that I lit three of them all simultaneously in an attempt to form a large fireball. Nagoyan scolded me for wastefulness.

I squatted and gazed at them, wondering what tomorrow would bring.

I dunno. What'll 'appen? I dunno. What'll 'appen?

When the last of fireworks had faded, the sense of loneliness they had fleetingly dulled came rushing back.

"It's all my fault."

I had been trying to get to sleep without hearing those weird voices, when I heard Nagoyan calling out in the darkness.

"I should have stopped you. I thoughtlessly took the car and needlessly prevented your return... And where are we now in this absurd place? I even let you drive without a license. We'll be in a terrible pickle if we get caught... Your parents must hate me enough to kill me. When I get back, I'll be charged with kidnapping. It'll be called a case of abduction... Will I be able to get my job back? I suppose not... In the end, I'll be called in by the police after all..."

The longer I kept silent, the more Nagoyan went on grumbling, grumbling, grumbling. Even without any of that, I was covered in sticky sweat, and the more Nagoyan went on, the more humid it became. I raised my seat and said, "T'isn't so bad as ye think. Drink yer Depas."

"I've already taken it."

His voice sounded shrill in my ears. I daubed Sea Breeze on the nape of my neck and on my arms and furiously waved my fan, unable otherwise to endure the muggy heat of the night.

"If you think you can solve all your problems with drugs, you're dead wrong. That's your biggest mistake."

"But if I don't take me meds, I'll never git well."

"You've been taking it all along, but it doesn't seem to have done you much good, has it?"

"I'll git well someday, I will. It's only that Tetropin that I really hate."

"Listen. You're forever talking about running away, running away, but in fact we're doing just the opposite. Aren't we simply letting ourselves be herded in? Why didn't we head toward Honshu? Wait a minute. We were supposed to get on the expressway at Dazaifu... And this is how it's turned out. So look. It's like this. Running away doesn't make things any better."

"In that prison we woulda gone totally off our rockers. We're better off as we are."

"So that's why I'm asking – are we to just keep on going? What're you going to do when you run out of medicine?" Nagoyan asked shrilly.

"We're not really running away, though, are we? There's no road fer it!"

I thought he was on the verge of tears.

"An' aren't ye the one who's been runnin' away from Nagoya?"

My voice was lower than usual. The strange thing was that the more Nagoyan raged, the calmer I became. I didn't itch, and I didn't hear "Twenty..."

"Mind your own business! I wasn't running away from Nagoya. I *dumped* Nagoya."

"Even if ye did, ye can ne'er quite git away. 'Tis the same thing as bein' on Planet Earth: there's no escape."

"I don't know what you're talking about," he replied weepily.

"Ye can take a flyin' leap into space to git away, but gravity will still pull ye back. An' people who try to do that are jus' plain daft. But then I'm one of 'em an' so are ye."

I was hardly thinking as I spoke, sputtering incoherently, a player piano hammering the keys. My tone was calm, but I was talking gibberish, and I knew it.

"Do you suppose it's like being a mullet?"

In my mind I saw those huge fish leaping out of the mouth of the Hiikawa and splashing back in again. Anyone who's done a bellyflop would think that hitting the surface like that must be painful, but the mullet are a thick-skinned, insensitive lot and may not feel it. Or perhaps they can't help jumping, even if it hurts. Without asking one of them, I wouldn't know.

"Aye," I replied, "like a mullet…" For a long time he said nothing.

"…We're low on gasoline. Wonder how much longer we can go. If we wind up with an empty tank here in the mountains, we'll really be stuck… I wonder if any bears will come prowling around… If we're this hungry, I can imagine that they are… Oh, if only we could get the air conditioner fixed…"

Nagoyan had started his grumbling again. I closed my eyes. Then finally, as though he had completed his quotidian quota of chatter, he fell silent, and so the day was now truly at an end. I quickly fell into a pitch-black sleep.

12

——

I had been close to despair about what lay in store for us, but the next morning, as we came over the prefectural border into Kumamoto, the road substantially improved. Yielding to us as we passed were cars with local license plates, going goodness knows where. We steadily descended along a stream, passing by a cement factory with a number of mixing trucks parked in front, where, off to the side, we saw a service station – a distinctly minor, makeshift facility, I should say, without even so much as a vending machine.

"What is the best way to get to Kobayashi?" Nagoyan asked the middle-aged proprietor, who pointed to the narrow road across the way.

"Tha's a shortcut. 'Tis the long way roun' if ye go through Taragi." He gave the car's license plate a curious glance.

"Yer from Nagoya then."

"Uh, yes," replied Nagoyan perfunctorily. He did not claim to be from Tokyo.

"From Shiiba we tried to go to Miyazaki."

"It musta been terrible," the man said with a laugh. "It's a wretched road!"

Nagoyan was not being his usually affable self. He turned to the proprietor, who was taking his time filling the tank, and asked in a shrill voice, "Where are we anyway?"

"In Tsukigi."

He gave a complicated explanation of how the characters were written and then pointed to a sign on the cement factory where the name could be seen.

"Would there be any place 'ere where we might get sumptin' to eat?" I asked, trying to get a word in edgewise.

"In Kobayashi ye can get anythin' ye want."

With the tank full, we put Tsukigi behind us, still not knowing where it was.

We hadn't driven for an hour before the landscape opened up to broad paddy fields. It was good to see signs of human agricultural activity. The rice plants had grown and now, still green, had sprouted ears. Soon the entire scene would turn to gold, and then there would something delicious to savor. I was hungry. In the distance I glimpsed the real Mount Kirishima; there were also farmhouses and traffic lights. Vehicles and roads were gathering from all directions; we had entered the town of Kobayashi. It was a town all right, but one that seemed to have lost all track of time. Hardly any of the sunburned, faded buildings were more than two stories high. The shop selling daily necessities resembled a crude storage shed. I was somewhat disappointed. The only edifice that stood out was the brightly colored service station.

The sky abruptly turned dark and we were hit by a passing shower. Nagoyan grinned, saying that now we would at least get relief from the heat, but when we closed the windows, the discomfort index became relentlessly worse, until, with the mixed odor of two unrelated persons' sweat, it was all quite unendurable. We turned around and went back. Giving up on the idea of Hyuga chicken, we went into Joyful to kill time until the rain stopped. I had a hamburger, Nagoyan an assortment of fried food. We were out of sorts, but at least we were getting something to eat. I kept going to the drink bar for iced coffee refills, despite Nagoyan's expressed concerns that such would only put me in need of a restroom. *Who cares?* I thought to myself. *When yer this deep into the countryside, ye can jus' pee in th' bushes.*

The breeze that came with the letup of the rain was not we had hoped for. We made a halfhearted effort to ventilate the car.

"Isn't it about time for a change of drivers?" Nagoyan asked. "You should be able to handle this stretch of road."

"Ye should be doin' the drivin', Nagoyan. Ye're so much better at it."

"Hey, don't you realize that I've been behind the wheel for hundreds of kilometers now? Why can't you at least say 'thank you' or 'sorry'?"

There was again a tone of hysteria in his voice. He suddenly turned on the heater.

"What're ye doin'? Are ye hatterin' me?"

I was furious.

"Take it easy, will you? The water temperature's going up."

I didn't know what he was talking about and thought that, if I asked, all I'd get was a convoluted answer.

You tell me you've been hurt, but it's a lie.
You tell me I should hang in there, but I just can't.
Don't you be a goody two-shoes.
Don't you be a goody two-shoes.

"I'm sorry... Pull in there."

In a bad mood, I marched into an old, foul-smelling liquor store and brazenly shoplifted a bottle of Myers's Rum. Whether I put it into a shopping basket or stuffed it into my tote bag didn't make a lot of difference. I returned in triumph to the passenger seat, deftly opened the bottle, and took a swig. In my throat and at the back of my eyes, I felt the heat of the liquid.

"Hey! No drinking in the passenger seat!"

"I'll do whit I bloody well like!"

Nagoyan clicked his tongue and pressed his foot to the accelerator.

"Hand it over!" he shouted, grabbed the bottle, and took a large gulp.

"Whooh!" he gasped.

"Prior to the Second World War, condemned prisoners about to be sent to the gallows would, after prayers, be given a glass of rum."

So saying, he glugged down some more. Not to be bested, I grabbed the bottle back and took another swallow myself.

"Are ye awright for drivin'?" I asked him.

"Who knows? I'm fine with it. After all, I've been doing it every day now."

He turned up the sound of the car stereo and then, without warning, suddenly put on the brakes, got out, and went over to a vending machine to buy several cans of Coke.

"Let's have some Cuba libre."

"Whit's that?"

"It means 'free Cuba'. You take Cuban rum and mix it with Coca-Cola from America, which symbolizes freedom. But the Americans call it rum and coke. And now that I've mentioned Cuba, I'm reminded that there's a book about Che Guevara that's come out recently. I wanted to read it."

"I haven't a clue whit ye're talkin' about."

I'd really had my fill of Nagoyan's pointless arguments. We'd gone over hill and dale, but there seemed to be not a single lavender field anywhere in Kyushu. And it was futile to go looking for one. I said nothing and kept drinking. And then I felt sick. I asked Nagoyan to stop the car. He pulled into a parking area with no toilet. I went into the bushes and vomited my hamburger and rum, then dizzily made my way back. From the window on the driver's side, Nagoyan violently threw the empty bottle toward the road. I heard the crashing sound, as it burst, the shards sparkling as they scattered.

"I wish I could go to pieces in the same way!" he remarked softly, though it was as though he had spat the words out. After that we were both silent.

13

———

Roaring along as though we were on the Nijo-hamatama expressway, we headed toward Miyazaki on Route 268, a road which, though entirely carved through the mountains, nonetheless had a yellow line running down the exact middle of it.

The city suddenly appeared. As we came down a gentle slope in the direction of the river, it was glimmering from the other side like a mirage.

"Wow!" both of us simultaneously exclaimed. It was as though we had in an instant sobered up. My foul mood and Nagoyan's irritation had been swept away.

"'Tis a real city!"

"There are buildings… *buildings!*"

"7-Eleven!"

"Ah, there's a Royal Host!"

We called out with each such discovery, guffawing with glee.

"Where have we come from?!"

"Seems like Miyazaki's awright. I thought it'd be quite rustic."

"I had no idea it would be such an exciting place!"

The next instant, I gave a shout, even as Nagoyan wrenched the steering wheel around. "A Mazda dealer!"

Nagoyan carefully edged his "Hiroshima Mercedes" right into the middle of the rows of new red and silver vehicles in the parking lot and stopped. He handed the key to a mechanic, and we then waited in the air-conditioned, glass-paneled showroom, looking at the shiny cars.

"They ain't got any new Luces?"

"They haven't been making them for some time now."

"Is that so?"

I was beginning to feel an affectionate attachment to the square-shaped car. So they didn't make them anymore… A pity. We sat in the leather chairs used by customers when negotiating with the sales agents. What would we do if we had to cool our heels for several days or even a week? I didn't feel in any particular hurry; I had no sense of being pursued. But I still didn't want to be stuck there.

The mechanic returned sooner than we expected.

The hose, he explained, had a hole in it, the result of the usual wear and tear, so that the gas had leaked out. He'd repaired it and put in new gas. As he was clearly from the southern part of the island, even I could barely understand him

Rolling his eyes, Nagoyan interrupted, "So it's all right then?"

"Aye," the man went on but said that if we had let it go, we might have wound up having oil leaking onto the compressor and burning, and that would have required more time and money.

All Nagoyan heard was "Aye." "Good!" he exclaimed, breathing a deep sigh of relief. I didn't really understand what the two were talking about, but was glad that it was nothing really dreadful.

The Luce was waiting for us at the exit, the air conditioner humming away in fine form. It seemed to be saying, "I still have some life in me!" I thought that as it was a product of Hiroshima, it ought to be speaking the dialect there. But then I wouldn't have understood it.

"Wow! It's cool!"

"Enough t' give ye goosebumps!"

We were back in high-tension mode.

We had no need at this point for the fast track and so drove on past the Eastern Kyushu Expressway interchange, quite ignoring it. Nagoyan drove into a shopping district along Route 10. Pulling up to the walkway in front of a most attractive building, he stopped the car.

"Let's stay here."

It was a hotel, with the emblem of Japan Airlines on display. As we walked in, I was enveloped by a sudden coolness, so different from all we had been experiencing. Nagoyan walked up to the receptionist and leaned his elbow on the counter, quite as though we had come into a shot bar.

"Two double rooms."

I said bye-bye to Nagoyan as I went into the room next to his. I opened the door and saw that it was tastefully arranged, with a lowboy, an oval table, and, most importantly, a double bed. Drinking in the joy of having it all to myself, I threw myself onto the firm, broad mattress. Until the morning, this room would be mine.

But then, when I had undressed and gone into the immaculate bathroom, turned the shiny faucets, and felt the strong spray of the shower, I remembered the low water level in the reservoir that we had left behind that morning. The naïve pleasure of brushing up against civilization is indeed short-lived.

The towels were thick and snowy white. I wanted to steal them. Thievery had now become second nature to me, and here there was everything. There were toothbrushes and coffee. Nagoyan could even turn over to a laundry service the same clothes he had risked his life to wash himself.

I put on the vertically striped, turquoise nightshirt and, like a slice of sandwiched ham, got in between the well-starched sheets of the snugly made bed. I wondered whether a baby kangaroo still longs for its mother's pouch even after it's grown up.

Lying there, staring up at the pure white ceiling, I reflected that the day I would lose Nagoyan was probably near. He was not the sort of person to hang about in Kyushu forever. I would deliberately use Saga dialect as I said goodbye. Nagoyan would then know my meaning. Not that it would matter much...

I hadn't taken any medication, but as I was mulling everything over, I drowsed off. Two hours later, I awoke and happily thought about all the time I could still spend in the room. I watched a bit of TV and was relieved to see that there was no news about any search for us. The Fukuoka Daiei Hawks had won three games in a row. I downed my barbiturates with beer and fell into a deep sleep.

I was startled awake by the ring of the telephone. It was morning. I hoped that the call was from neither my parents nor the police.

"Were you asleep?" It was Nagoyan's voice.

"Jus' woke up."

"I slept soundly too. Let's have some breakfast and then go shopping."

The tone of his voice was buoyant. I bundled out of bed.

"Aye, I'll git ready!"

Nagoyan was waiting for me, sitting on a black leather sofa in the lobby, wearing the polo shirt he had washed in the river and puffing away on a Salem Light, something he normally did only just before bedtime. We took full advantage of the hotel's buffet breakfast and then popped off into the brilliant light of Miyazaki's shopping district. The sunlight was indeed brighter than in Fukuoka, beaming directly down on us.

"Is there something you particularly want?"

"Whit about ye?"

"I've been needing to buy some clothes."

"I'd like to take a peek at Prada."

"I'll buy you something."

"No thanks. It's aw too dear. It'll be fun jus' to window-shop."

"We can use all this money. I don't think I'll be buying a Porsche anyway."

Hearing the word "Porsche," I was reminded of our hit-and-run experience in Aso, but then thought that the man and his moll wouldn't be on our trail. We were far away, and the car in question had had Chikuho plates.

Nagoyan, having bought a Brooks Brothers shirt, was in an expansive mood, saying we should now head for Prada. For the first time in quite a while, he was having fun just strolling through the streets.

I wanted a Prada bag. After our miserable odyssey, I wanted what for once would be a happy souvenir. I wanted something to remind me, with whomever I might travel in the future, of this particular journey. But then I immediately sensed that it was all self-deception, that I merely wanted a present to console me for the loss of Nagoyan.

"I've changed me mind. I don't want it."

"Why?"

"It's awright."

"After going to all the trouble…" exclaimed Nagoyan with an air of dissatisfaction. "Well then, at least put on some makeup. After all, we're here in town."

Nagoyan took me to Yamakataya, where there was a complete assortment of Max Factor products. The saleswoman helped give me a "natural" look. As it was Nagoyan who was watching the process and not a female friend, I felt awkward, embarrassed, bedazzled. The last time I had worn makeup was before being hospitalized, and that had been so long ago that I couldn't remember exactly when it was.

"Fine," said Nagoyan as he saw the result. "Now then, let's have a bit of a timeout and meet up again in the hotel lobby at seven."

"We're to stay ower then?"

"Yes, let's do that. One night's not enough to deal with our fatigue." So saying, he happily disappeared into the back streets.

Having nothing else to do, I wandered about the arcade, went into a bookstore where I bought a magazine and then went into a Mister Donut for a cup of coffee. I was feeling quite normal, with no hint of the voice. I'd lost track of where I was.

Back at the hotel, I took a most luxurious bath. Hot springs are pleasant too, but in this private bath, I could relax. In this intimate solitude, there was no need to engage in conversation with anyone.

At seven, having put on my makeup, I went down to the lobby, where I found Nagoyan waiting for me; he was dressed in his new button-down shirt and had even had his hair cut. We went into the restaurant for dinner. Was this all some sort of mistake? Was everything that had happened so far a mistake? That we had escaped from the hospital and were now contentedly enjoying a French course menu – was *that* a mistake? If we had been in Fukuoka, it might have been otherwise, but now here in my mouth was unmistakably the roast Hyuga chicken of which I had dreamt at the Tashirobae Dam.

"Did you know that from here you can take a ferry to Kawasaki?"

"Nope."

And I had no wish to take that ferry. For some reason, my ardor for escape had cooled. Nagoyan likewise seemed to have no particular attachment to Kawasaki.

"It's been a while since I've seen the necktie crowd." Nagoyan's expression slightly clouded over. "They must come here a lot on business. The airport is close."

"An' if ye fly, ye ha no trouble gettin' to Tokyo."

"No. The distance from Tokyo to Fukuoka is more than twice the distance from Fukuoka to Tokyo."

"Huh? It's no th' same?"

"It feels longer."

"Aye."

"My ex told me when I got transferred to Kyushu that she felt sorry for me being sent off to bumpkinsville. And it was a bit of shock all right."

"How can ye call Fukuoka anythin' but urban? If it's bumpkinsville ye want…"

The rest went without saying, as we were probably both thinking of the nightmarish road we had recently driven.

"Tokyoites don't see Fukuoka in particular; they see Kyushu as a whole. From their point of view, it's like a foreign country. I hate to admit it, but that's the way I thought too, and so I understand the mentality."

Yet, in so saying, he was as much as conceding that he was now himself a semi-Fukuokan.

"So yer ex was misled."

"Yes, she had it wrong. But so what? It can't be helped."

Human beings see what they want to see. Nagoyan had told me that, and I wondered whether that might be true. I had no desire to give Nagoyan's ex a tour of Fukuoka. It occurred to me that I would have happily dumped her at Tashirobae Dam. I also realized that I had missed the chance to ask Nagoyan whether his Nurse Shimada looked like her.

14

———

I felt somehow heavyhearted as we left Miyazaki. Route 10 to
Kagoshima was flat, with nothing unusual about it. Kyushu's
mountainous terrain had come to an end.

The ballad began at a leisurely pace, with soft, deep rumble of a
bass, like a 4B lead pencil, with the heartbreaking sound of a guitar
shimmering in the light.

> There is nothing to say;
> I'll not be going home.
> The dying day
> As I walked with her,
> Gazing at the river,
> A train passing over the bridge...

The cold spring water at the train crossing in South Aso was again
coursing through me. Slow, penetrating...

"I like this ballad."

> Though the day was dying
> I walked with her;
> Though the day was dying
> I walked with her.

Blood was flowing through that reckless man. His bluntness had a
gentle tone, as though to say that it is all right to weep.

> All, whatever their appearance,
> Have vanished one by one.
> And at the very end

We two long remained
Until we grew weary as well.

Would Nagoyan, in some time yet to come, be walking with her
at the end of the day through the streets of Tokyo, streets unknown
to me? *Had he done so before?* And at that time, would all that was
happening now be quite gone from my mind?

I need nothing;
I need nothing else.
As long as she's there…
Though the day was dying
I walked with her;
Though the day was dying
I walked with her.

"In the live version, it goes, 'Even as I was freaking out, I walked
with her'."
This was our song. I rewound the tape again and again and listened
to it.
Such was my mood. I was happy to listen to it all the way to
Kagoshima. It was just the right tune for this beat-up old car. And,
slowly but surely, even talking was becoming irksome, for I could see
the dead end looming before us. And beyond that lay depression. I
quickly picked up the song and sang my own words.

I sing 'cos it's hot; I sing 'cos I'm scared.
Twenty yards of linen are worth one coat.
Even as I was freaking out, I walked with her.

The sky before us was clouded over. I realized later that this was not
due to the weather, but rather to the volcanic smoke of Sakurajima.
The mountain was slumping into the sea. From the streets of
Kagoshima across the bay came flickering reflections of light. Even
from that distance, I was struck by how large the provincial capital
was. And yet, the excitement I had felt at seeing Miyazaki was not
there. Something rather significant seemed to be missing.

We rode in air-conditioned silence into the city. It certainly had a grand appearance, with many more imposing buildings than we saw in Miyazaki. There were bronze statues all around and rows of neatly trimmed, bonsai-like trees. Despite all of our foolishness, the life of the community was proceeding quite normally.

"Look at all the white cars!"

"Oh?"

"I've heard that with all the volcanic ash that falls, black cars don't sell. I wonder if we'll get any today..."

"Not in th' summer, I s'pose. The direction of the wind changes wi' th' season."

Years before, while still a child, I had heard about Kagoshima from my Aunt Yasuko. She was herself from the city. My mother's younger brother, my Uncle Toshi, had met and wed her years before when he was working there. I was trying to remember it all, when I heard Nagoyan shriek. (I mused whether there was any day in the year that he didn't shriek at least once.)

"Whit is it wit' ye now?"

"My company! The Kagoshima branch."

"Where?"

Out of the corner of my eye I saw the mark for Nippon Telegraph and Telephone.

"Whit o' it?!"

"Well, wouldn't it give you the jitters? Everybody working as usual, while we..."

"While ye're getting' yerself drowned and pishin' in yer breekums?"

"Never mind," replied Nagoyan sullenly. But he had clearly lost his high spirits. We passed Kagoshima University, and though I might have ignored them, the sight of the campus and the students caused me to fall into a funk as well. There they were, going to school as usual, chatting about their love lives or their part-time jobs.

How stupid it all seemed. And yet that kind of life, which we had put behind us, now lay once again in full view.

Our parents, the hospital, and the police would be still looking for us, but none of these people here would know our faces. The odd-looking Luce with its Nagoya license plate would probably arouse no attention. We were, to be sure, missing persons, but still somehow getting by.

And yet, I thought of at least calling my parents sometime.

We continued on through the city streets, still traveling the national highway. I gently mumbled that this way was leading to the end, but all he did was sing – in a somewhat hoarse voice – "Love is Blue."

At Ibusuki, we went into a hot springs. The water was quite hot, so I made quick work of it and returned to the changing room, where I wondered, as I luxuriated in front of the electric fan, whether Aunt Yasuko had come from here. She died when I was still in middle school, so I don't remember her very well, though I do know that she always spoke to me in standard speech. At the time, it had seemed refined and elegant. She told me that there was near her native town a mysterious island to which one could only cross when the tide was out.

"And then the sea makes way for a sandy pathway that one can walk. Let's go there some day!"

"Like Umi-no-Nakamichi in Fukuoka?"

"Umi-no-Nakamichi is a broad and splendid road running through the sea, isn't it? I'm talking about a narrow sand path that's almost always buried under the water. It's rare that we can walk it."

I wrote an essay about that when I was in the fourth year of primary school, but Kagoshima was far away, and my aunt died before we could go there together. I wondered whether the place she was talking about was nearby.

I called out resolutely to the man fanning himself at the reception desk, "Is there not a place near here where ye can walk ower the sand t' an island?"

He told me, speaking in Kagoshima dialect, that I must be thinking of Chirin-ga-shima.

"Yes, yes. Is it far?"

"No", he said. "Quite close." I was to turn just before the national recreational village, and as it was just half-tide, I wouldn't have any trouble.

I thanked him in a loud voice and bowed. "'Tis nuthin'," he replied.

There was indeed a sand path, formed like a gently curving S, that led to a green island shaped like a beret tossed onto the sea, with a slight indentation in the middle.

"If you built a castle here," remarked Nagoyan, "it would look like Mont St. Michel."

The sensation of walking on top of the sea was quite pleasant, but it was nonetheless hot. The heat seemed to bear down like searing, transparent crystals, penetrating the skull.

"Eeeeh!"

Nagoyan had screeched again. I looked and saw lying in the sand a dead starfish some twenty-five centimeters in diameter.

Gazing toward the Kagoshima side of the sea that was now partitioned by the sand path, I saw rising up into the offing something resembling a yellowish ball.

"Whit's that?"

Nagoyan too let out an exclamation, as he turned to look. The ball disappeared, then reappeared, popping up out of the water. It was moving in our direction. I could make out a bald head and then realized that the swimming form was that of a sea goblin.

In the shallows, which went on for a remarkable distance, the goblin now stood straight up and walked toward us, swaying its arms back and forth as it parted the waves. Though hardly tall, it seemed to have no trace of body fat – a real six-pack – and had a chiseled face. It was wearing dazzlingly crimson swimming trunks, so that when the waves receded, bringing its nether region into view, I didn't know where to look. Nagoyan glanced at me, as though to plead "What are we to do?" but as our eyes had met, I thought that we would have to exchange greetings. The goblin – or I should now say Red Trunks, a *yokanise*, all right – came closer, then looking directly at us, asked, "Let me take your photo."

There was no salutation, no inquiry as to where we had come from.

"Photo?"

In echoing the question, Nagoyan sounded as though his voice were emanating from the crown of his head. I responded that we hadn't any camera.

To my surprise, the *yokanise* produced from a mountain of clothes he had piled next to the dead starfish, a throwaway.

"Let's use this to get you two on film."

"But ye've other photos on it."

"Only the local scenery. And that's something we've always got."

So saying, the *yokanise* had us stand with the island in the background.

"Here we go: one, two, three…" He pressed the shutter.

"How about one with you too?"

Before I could get the words out, the man had, with a grin, wound the film and offered the camera to Nagoyan.

"Really…?"

"The sun's strong, so be careful."

We bade him farewell and continued on our way to the island.

"A bit of an odd character," whispered Nagoyan.

"Ye call a man like that a *yokanise*."

"What's that?"

"That's the local word fer a hunk"

It was one of the few words of the dialect that I knew.

"Eh? Is he your type, Hana-chan?"

Nagoyan was rolling with laughter.

"No, no!" I blushingly protested, but Nagoyan went on laughing as far as the island.

The way across the tiny beach of Chirin-ga-shima abruptly ended with a cliff covered in tall grass; there was no path to the other side. At the edge of the beach was a gray rock bulging into the sea. It seemed to me that the entire area had been sealed off.

"Is this all there is?"

"It'd seem so."

"So we can't go onto the island."

"'Tis a dead-end."

"Hmm. So it is."

"We have no choice but t' turn aboot."

The way back was nothing but long and hot. The starfish was still lying dead where we had seen it, but there was no sign of the hunk in his red trunks. Now that I thought about it, I realized that while he had had his clothes there, he was without a towel. An odd thing to remember.

"Here it was, wasn't it?"

Nagoyan was also thinking of the man.

"Say!"

It was only for an instant, but I detected a fragrance, a strong fragrance.

"Now that's a pleasant scent!" said Nagoyan.

"Lavender!"

"It's lavender!"

Wafting across the path where no a single blade of grass grew was the distinct scent of lavender.

I stood motionless, deeply breathing in the fragrance I had yearned so long for.

"Hana-chan, the tide's coming in."

If Nagoyan hadn't said that, I might have remained there forever.

The sandbar had waned to a mere sliver, as the sea moved from both sides to reclaim it. We quickened our pace in the burning sun and at last completed the last leg back. Reaching solid ground, we glanced back: the waves had washed away our path.

"It's quite gone," said Nagoyan.

"It's time we were goin' back," I declared. It was the first time I had uttered the idea. Nagoyan responded only with a tight-mouthed nod. When we came to the traffic light that would put us on the national highway, he remarked, "But this isn't the end of our journey, is it?"

"Don'cha wanna go as far as the Satsuma Peninsula?"

It occurred to me that it was there that I wished to bid farewell to the departing summer.

15

—

"Since leaving Fukuoka," announced Nagoyan with an air of pride, "we've gone over the one thousand kilometer mark." We had just stopped the car at the Nagasaki-bana Parking Garden. There were phoenixes all around us.

"Whit's a thousand kilometers?"

"A flight from Tokyo to Fukuoka covers nine hundred kilometers; by car on the expressways it's probably a bit more."

There was no time to give the matter any thought, for at that very instant, I was startled by a screech, followed by a responding screech. Coming toward us were two garish birds, each with a red head, a green body, and a blue tail. We were obviously in the tropics.

"Parrots?"

"It says here that they're macaws."

To get to the sea we had to cross the jungle park, where we came to the zoo. Kept here were animals ranging from the ring-tailed lemur to white snakes. And they all were emitting a horrible stench. Nagoyan, something of a cursorial bird himself, was unbelievably buoyant, calling out "Come on! Come on!" to each and every horrible beast. For a hundred yen he purchased some feed and offered it to a particularly heinous bird that looked as though it were descended from the pterosaur. When an ostrich three times my size came toward us leisurely swaying its feathers, and, with a speed amazing for its bulk, poked at Nagoyan's hand and snatched away the food, I naturally let out a screech of my own. For his part, Nagoyan was not the least frightened. He didn't scream or shout; he merely laughed. What was he about?

At last we came through the park and came out on the cape. Suddenly we could hear pulsating through us the sound of waves. The water was bluer than that of either the Genkai Sea or Bungo

Channel on the northern coasts. The mightiest of the seas we had seen on our journey was here.

When we got down to the beach, we could see the green form of Kaimondake rising straight up from across the small bay. All the way to the peak the view was cloudlessly clear, the beckoningly beautiful ridgeline distinct and solidly real, as though seen in a pencil sketch.

"What's that?" shrieked Nagoyan in his high-pitched voice. "Is it a replica of Mt. Fuji?"

"Tha's Kaimondake, the Mt. Fuji o' Satsuma."

I'd only seen the real Mt. Fuji twice, but the one here was vastly more elegant, imposing, bountiful...rising gallantly out of the sea and towering over all.

"Why is it shaped like that?"

"Dunno. Ye'd hafta ask the mountain."

"I never imagined that when we reached the land's end we'd be in for a sight like this."

Nagoyan was fit to be tied. I could see clearly how furious he was at seeing his beloved mountain put to shame.

The black sand was hot and crumbly. We walked to the sea and back. Feeling the grit in my shoes, I sat down at the edge of the walkway and shook them out, breathing softly, embraced in the twilight that was already beginning to fall.

"Twenty yards of linen..."

I thought it was in my head, but it was actually my own voice. I could no longer hear G. It was a sentence I no longer needed to hear. The Limas were working.

"Ah, such a feeling of *yutaa!*"

"Huh?" Nagoyan was still standing, glaring at Kaimondake.

"Ye don't git it?"

His failure to understand such important concepts was irksome...

"Oh, all right. Now I know what you're talking about... Relaxing..."

"If ye put it *that* way," I said somewhat coldly, "the mood will slip away."

Yutaa is about wanting to embrace the whole world – and to have the whole world embrace me in return, as I let my whole body unwind and my feeling of "being alive" becomes overwhelmingly good. And yet, saying such would only cause the wings of Nagoyan's nose to twitch, as he held forth tediously on the blah-blah "nature of existence."

So I kept my *yutaa* to myself and merely asked, "Whit day is it? Wonder how long we've been on the run..."

"September eighteenth." Nagoyan looked at his watch to make sure. "Actually, today was to be the date of my release."

This was the first I'd heard of it. If he'd told me the day of our escape, I wouldn't have brought him along. Once quite well, he could have left the hospital and gone back to work, neatly dressed in a suit and tie. If I hadn't talked a lot of rot, there wouldn't have been the slightest need for him to come this far with me. There were, to be sure, those recovering from depression who experienced suicidal impulses, but Nagoyan would probably have been like the many patients able to overcome these. It was all my fault. And during all this time we had been together, he had said nothing. He had not once reproved me for that. In the depths of my heart I felt for the first time a genuine sense of remorse.

"I'm sorry, Nagoyan. I'm truly sorry."

I bowed and looked up again to see him slowly shaking his head.

"Never mind. It's all right. What about Makurazaki? Do you want to go there later?"

"It doesn't matter now."

"I'm really tired all right," he remarked with a grin.

"Aye."

From time to time there were dark swells in the open sea, the light reflecting off the back of the shifting billows and stinging our eyes. Huge waves were sporadically crashing white against the rocks at the base of a lighthouse.

"Shall we go back?"

"Aye."

"You're lucky. You can go back to where you were born in Hakata."

I had never thought otherwise. I wouldn't have understood that if I hadn't met Nagoyan, with all his mixed feelings of love for his birthplace.

For some moments I gazed at him in profile and then deliberately asked, "Won't it be good ta get home t' Gokuraku?"

I had only intended to tease him a bit, but the upper part of his face now became dizzyingly distorted. He descended to the beach. Stumbling as he faced the clear outline of Satsuma's Mt. Fuji across the blue sea, he shouted, "Not on yar bloody loony life!"